MORA

THE CONDAMINE CASE

KATHERINE DALTON RENOIR ('Moray Dalton') was born in Hammersmith, London in 1881, the only child of a Canadian father and English mother.

The author wrote two well-received early novels, *Olive in Italy* (1909), and *The Sword of Love* (1920). However, her career in crime fiction did not begin until 1924, after which Moray Dalton published twenty-nine mysteries, the last in 1951. The majority of these feature her recurring sleuths, Scotland Yard inspector Hugh Collier and private inquiry agent Hermann Glide.

Moray Dalton married Louis Jean Renoir in 1921, and the couple had a son a year later. The author lived on the south coast of England for the majority of her life following the marriage. She died in Worthing, West Sussex, in 1963.

MORAY DALTON MYSTERIES
Available from Dean Street Press

One by One They Disappeared
The Night of Fear
The Body in the Road
Death in the Cup
The Strange Case of Harriet Hall
The Belfry Murder
The Belgrave Manor Crime
The Case of Alan Copeland
The Art School Murders
The Condamine Case

MORAY DALTON

THE CONDAMINE CASE

With an introduction by Curtis Evans

DEAN STREET PRESS

LOST GOLD FROM A GOLDEN AGE

The Detective Fiction of Moray Dalton
(Katherine Mary Deville Dalton Renoir, 1881-1963)

"GOLD" COMES in many forms. For literal-minded people gold may be merely a precious metal, physically stripped from the earth. For fans of Golden Age detective fiction, however, gold can be artfully spun out of the human brain, in the form not of bricks but books. While the father of Katherine Mary Deville Dalton Renoir may have derived the Dalton family fortune from nuggets of metallic ore, the riches which she herself produced were made from far humbler, though arguably ultimately mightier, materials: paper and ink. As the mystery writer Moray Dalton, Katherine Dalton Renoir published twenty-nine crime novels between 1924 and 1951, the majority of which feature her recurring sleuths, Scotland Yard inspector Hugh Collier and private inquiry agent Hermann Glide. Although the Moray Dalton mysteries are finely polished examples of criminally scintillating Golden Age art, the books unjustifiably fell into neglect for decades. For most fans of vintage mystery they long remained, like the fabled Lost Dutchman's mine, tantalizingly elusive treasure. Happily the crime fiction of Moray Dalton has been unearthed for modern readers by those industrious miners of vintage mystery at Dean Street Press.

Born in Hammersmith, London on May 6, 1881, Katherine was the only child of Joseph Dixon Dalton and Laura Back Dalton. Like the parents of that admittedly more famous mistress of mystery, Agatha Christie, Katherine's parents hailed from different nations, separated by the Atlantic Ocean. While both authors had British mothers, Christie's father was American and Dalton's father Canadian.

Laura Back Dalton, who at the time of her marriage in 1879 was twenty-six years old, about fifteen years younger than her husband, was the daughter of Alfred and Catherine Mary Back. In her early childhood years Laura Back resided at Valley House, a lovely regency villa built around 1825 in Stratford St. Mary, Suffolk, in the heart of so-called "Constable Country" (so named for the fact that the great Suffolk landscape artist John Constable painted many of his works in and around Stratford). Alfred Back was a wealthy miller who with his brother Octavius, a corn merchant, owned and operated a steam-powered six-story mill right across the River Stour from Valley House. In 1820 John Constable, himself the son of a miller, executed a painting of fishers on the River Stour which partly included the earlier, more modest incarnation (complete with water wheel) of the Back family's mill. (This piece Constable later repainted under the title *The Young Waltonians*, one of his best known works.) After Alfred Back's death in 1860, his widow moved with her daughters to Brondesbury Villas in Maida Vale, London, where Laura in the 1870s met Joseph Dixon Dalton, an eligible Canadian-born bachelor and retired gold miner of about forty years of age who lived in nearby Kew.

Joseph Dixon Dalton was born around 1838 in London, Ontario, Canada, to Henry and Mary (Dixon) Dalton, Wesleyan Methodists from northern England who had migrated to Canada a few years previously. In 1834, not long before Joseph's birth, Henry Dalton started a soap and candle factory in London, Ontario, which after his death two decades later was continued, under the appellation Dalton Brothers, by Joseph and his siblings Joshua and Thomas. (No relation to the notorious "Dalton Gang" of

American outlaws is presumed.) Joseph's sister Hannah wed John Carling, a politician who came from a prominent family of Canadian brewers and was later knighted for his varied public services, making him Sir John and his wife Lady Hannah. Just how Joseph left the family soap and candle business to prospect for gold is currently unclear, but sometime in the 1870s, after fabulous gold rushes at Cariboo and Cassiar, British Columbia and the Black Hills of South Dakota, among other locales, Joseph left Canada and carried his riches with him to London, England, where for a time he enjoyed life as a gentleman of leisure in one of the great metropolises of the world.

Although Joshua and Laura Dalton's first married years were spent with their daughter Katherine in Hammersmith at a villa named Kenmore Lodge, by 1891 the family had moved to 9 Orchard Place in Southampton, where young Katherine received a private education from Jeanne Delport, a governess from Paris. Two decades later, Katherine, now 30 years old, resided with her parents at Perth Villa in the village of Merriott, Somerset, today about an eighty miles' drive west of Southampton. By this time Katherine had published, under the masculine-sounding pseudonym of Moray Dalton (probably a gender-bending play on "Mary Dalton") a well-received first novel, *Olive in Italy* (1909), a study of a winsome orphaned Englishwoman attempting to make her own living as an artist's model in Italy that possibly had been influenced by E.M. Forster's novels *Where Angels Fear to Tread* (1905) and *A Room with a View* (1908), both of which are partly set in an idealized Italy of pure gold sunlight and passionate love. Yet despite her accomplishment, Katherine's name had no occupation listed next it in the census two years later.

During the Great War the Daltons, parents and child, resided at 14 East Ham Road in Littlehampton, a seaside resort town located 19 miles west of Brighton. Like many other bookish and patriotic British women of her day, Katherine produced an effusion of memorial war poetry, including "To Some Who Have Fallen," "Edith Cavell," "Rupert Brooke," "To Italy" and "Mort Homme." These short works appeared in the *Spectator* and were reprinted during and after the war in George Herbert Clarke's *Treasury of War Poetry* anthologies. "To Italy," which Katherine had composed as a tribute to the beleaguered British ally after its calamitous defeat, at the hands of the forces of Germany and Austria-Hungary, at the Battle of Caporetto in 1917, even popped up in the United States in the "poet's corner" of the *United Mine Workers Journal*, perhaps on account of the poem's pro-Italy sentiment, doubtlessly agreeable to Italian miner immigrants in America.

Katherine also published short stories in various periodicals, including *The Cornhill Magazine*, which was then edited by Leonard Huxley, son of the eminent zoologist Thomas Henry Huxley and father of famed writer Aldous Huxley. Leonard Huxley obligingly read over--and in his words "plied my scalpel upon"--Katherine's second novel, *The Sword of Love*, a romantic adventure saga set in the Florentine Republic at the time of Lorenzo the Magnificent and the infamous Pazzi Conspiracy, which was published in 1920. Katherine writes with obvious affection for *il bel paese* in her first two novels and her poem "To Italy," which concludes with the ringing lines

> Greece was enslaved, and Carthage is but dust,
> But thou art living, maugre [i.e., in spite of] all thy
>   scars,
> To bear fresh wounds of rapine and of lust,
> Immortal victim of unnumbered wars.
> Nor shalt thou cease until we cease to be
> Whose hearts are thine, beloved Italy.

The author maintained her affection for "beloved Italy" in her later Moray Dalton mysteries, which include sympathetically-rendered Italian settings and characters.

Around this time Katherine in her own life evidently discovered romance, however short-lived. At Brighton in the spring of 1921, the author, now nearly 40 years old, wed a presumed Frenchman, Louis Jean Renoir, by whom the next year she bore her only child, a son, Louis Anthony Laurence Dalton Renoir. (Katherine's father seems to have missed these important developments in his daughter's life, apparently having died in 1918, possibly in the flu pandemic.) Sparse evidence as to the actual existence of this man, Louis Jean Renoir, in Katherine's life suggests that the marriage may not have been a successful one. In the 1939 census Katherine was listed as living with her mother Laura at 71 Wallace Avenue in Worthing, Sussex, another coastal town not far from Brighton, where she had married Louis Jean eighteen years earlier; yet he is not in evidence, even though he is stated to be Katherine's husband in her mother's will, which was probated in Worthing in 1945. Perhaps not unrelatedly, empathy with what people in her day considered unorthodox sexual unions characterizes the crime fiction which Katherine would write.

Whatever happened to Louis Jean Renoir, marriage and motherhood did not slow down "Moray Dalton." Indeed, much to the contrary, in 1924, only a couple of years after the birth of her son, Katherine published, at the age of 42 (the same age at which P.D. James published her debut mystery novel, *Cover Her Face*), *The Kingsclere Mystery*, the first of her 29 crime novels. (Possibly the title was derived from the village of Kingsclere, located some 30 miles north of Southampton.) The heady scent of Renaissance romance which perfumes *The Sword of Love* is found as well in the first four Moray Dalton mysteries (aside from *The Kingsclere Mystery*, these are *The Shadow on the Wall*, *The Black Wings* and *The Stretton Darknesse Mystery*), which although set in the present-day world have, like much of the mystery fiction of John Dickson Carr, the elevated emotional temperature of the highly-colored age of the cavaliers. However in 1929 and 1930, with the publication of, respectively, *One by One They Disappeared*, the first of the Inspector Hugh Collier mysteries and *The Body in the Road*, the debut Hermann Glide tale, the Moray Dalton novels begin to become more typical of British crime fiction at that time, ultimately bearing considerable similarity to the work of Agatha Christie and Dorothy L. Sayers, as well as other prolific women mystery authors who would achieve popularity in the 1930s, such as Margery Allingham, Lucy Beatrice Malleson (best known as "Anthony Gilbert") and Edith Caroline Rivett, who wrote under the pen names E.C.R. Lorac and Carol Carnac.

For much of the decade of the 1930s Katherine shared the same publisher, Sampson Low, with Edith Rivett, who published her first detective novel in 1931, although Rivett moved on, with both of her pseudonyms, to that rather more prominent purveyor of mysteries, the Collins Crime Club. Consequently the Lorac and Carnac novels are better known today than those of Moray Dalton. Additionally, only three early Moray Dalton titles (*One by One They Disappeared*, *The Body in the Road* and *The Night of Fear*) were picked up in the United States, another factor which mitigated against the Dalton mysteries achieving long-term renown. It is also possible that the independently wealthy author, who left an estate valued, in modern estimation, at nearly a million American dollars at her death at the age of 81 in 1963, felt less of an imperative to "push" her writing than the typical "starving author."

Whatever forces compelled Katherine Dalton Renoir to write fiction, between 1929 and 1951 the author as Moray Dalton published fifteen Inspector Hugh Collier mysteries and ten other crime novels (several of these with Hermann Glide). Some of the non-series novels daringly straddle genres. *The Black Death*, for example, somewhat bizarrely yet altogether compellingly merges the murder mystery with post-apocalyptic science fiction, whereas *Death at the Villa*, set in Italy during the Second World War, is a gripping wartime adventure thriller with crime and death. Taken together, the imaginative and ingenious Moray Dalton crime fiction, wherein death is not so much a game as a dark and compelling human drama, is one of the more significant bodies of work by a Golden Age mystery writer—though the author has, until now, been most regrettably overlooked by publishers, for decades remaining accessible almost solely to connoisseurs with deep pockets.

Even noted mystery genre authorities Jacques Barzun and Wendell Hertig Taylor managed to read only five books by Moray Dalton, all of which the pair thereupon listed in their massive critical compendium, *A Catalogue of Crime* (1972; revised and expanded 1989). Yet Barzun and Taylor were warm admirers of the author's writing, avowing for example, of the twelfth Hugh Collier mystery, *The Condamine Case* (under the impression that the author was a man): "[T]his is the author's 17th book, and [it is] remarkably fresh and unstereotyped [actually it was Dalton's 25th book, making it even more remarkable—C.E.]. . . . [H]ere is a neglected man, for his earlier work shows him to be a conscientious workman, with a flair for the unusual, and capable of clever touches."

Today in 2019, nine decades since the debut of the conscientious and clever Moray Dalton's Inspector Hugh Collier detective series, it is a great personal pleasure to announce that this criminally neglected woman is neglected no longer and to welcome her books back into light. Vintage crime fiction fans have a golden treat in store with the classic mysteries of Moray Dalton.

The Condamine Case

"'Tes a queer place seemingly. . . . Full of ghostesses, what with beasts coming down from the church roof and her that walks up to Great Baring and her hair blowing like smoke in the gale. 'T'esn't a place to be out alone at night." Constable Puddock slowed down and sounded his horn as they came out into the road, and added rather hastily, "'Tes only old tales and ignorance."

The Condamine Case (1947), by Moray Dalton

IN MY introduction to Moray Dalton's *The Case of Alan Copeland* (1937), I write about how darkly Dalton portrayed the English village of Teene, with its monstrous regiment of women who might be seen as figurative "witches" of a sort, while in my introduction to Dalton's *The Art School Murders* (1943), I note how the author mentioned American films and Hollywood stars like Fred Astaire, Ginger Rogers and Robert Taylor. Well, in *The Condamine Case* we have actual witches, plus an English film crew making a movie involving witchcraft, at a remote English village, Little Baring in Somerset, apparently located somewhere in the vicinity of the actual village of Wookey (a name I had not, until reading this book, encountered outside of a Star Wars film). What fan of classic English mystery would want to miss this?

In London rising whiz kid director Stephen Latimer--he has been compared to no less than Orson Welles and René Clair, the latter of whom had recently directed the films *I Married a Witch* and *And Then There Were None* --learns of a gentry family in Somerset by the name of Condamine who have experienced a history of witchcraft and haunting. He decides this would make an excellent subject for his next film, so over he goes to the Condamine ancestral manor with his self-effacing assistant, Welshman Evan Hughes, the focal character of the novel, to scout out locations.

In Somerset Stephen and Evan stay at the imposing columned mansion of the Condamines: middle-aged husband George, who is desperately anxious that the film be made, and his beautiful, jaded younger wife of two years standing, Ida, who acts as though she is indifferent to the whole thing. Also integral members of the household are George's beloved old spaniel Punch and his ill-used young poor relation Lucy Arden, who serves as haughty Ida's beleaguered dogsbody.

According to legend, a seventeenth-century ancestor of George's kept a beautiful but humbly-born mistress in the village when he married a London heiress, and his jealous and vindictive new spouse saw to it that the mistress and her mother were accused of witchcraft and drowned (via the barbaric witch-revealing practice known as "ducking"). Unfortunately for the wife, the dead mistress returned from the dead as a ghost and haunted the wife unto her very death. All this supernatural legend material is well fashioned by the author, reminding me of those masters of spooky shudders John Dickson Carr and Marjorie Bowen (high praise indeed).

Stephen Latimer wants to spice things up yet more, however, by adding to the script the presence of England's notorious self-appointed seventeenth-century "witch-finder" (aka demented mass murderer) Matthew Hopkins, although Evan Hughes informs him that Hopkins never actually came near these parts. What British witchcraft film would not make use of such a splendid villain as Matthew Hopkins, however? Vincent Price would play him in the grim 1968 British film *Witchfinder General*, directed by Michael Reeves, who like the fictional Stephen Latimer was something of a directorial prodigy.

Moray Dalton knew southern England, her native ground, extremely well and in her novel she places a great deal of emphasis on the natural and man-made environment, which is based on real places in Somerset, like Glastonbury Tor, a conical hill steeped in history and legend, and the Church of St. Mary the Virgin at the village of Croscombe. Upon the latter location Dalton clearly based the Anglican Church at Little Baring. Standing before the church while scouting film locations, Evan is impressed by the bell tower's height as well as "the extraordinary and menacing effect produced by the multitude of carved stone gargoyles thrusting forward from the roof like the garrison of a fortress preparing to repel all comers. . . . horrid heads, grimacing, open-mouthed: giant lizards, pig snouts, figures from a nightmare, with scaly shoulders and outstretched sinewy necks and sharp talons gripping the eaves."

The eccentric bachelor rector of this memorable church, Sebastian Mallory, is another important figure in the novel's present day plot, as are George Condamine's bluntly garrulous widowed sister-in-law, Julia Condamine, and her indolent young adult son, Oswald ("Ozzie"). Since George married Ida, both Ozzie and Julia have been unhappily banished from the manor to a mere cottage (a picturesque one, to be sure).

Stephen and Evan leave Little Baring to return to London, but return with their actors and film crew a few months later, only to learn that Death has unexpectedly come calling in Little Baring. Soon there arrives upon the scene as well "a man of about fifty, with a slim, active-looking figure, hands tanned by the sun but noticeably well-kept, a lean brown face with shrewd grey eyes and a humorous mouth." Readers of the series will know who this is: Inspector Hugh Collier of the Yard, of course, in the crime detection game for nearly two decades now. With Collier comes his phlegmatic assistant of many years, Sergeant Duffield. Together they face a case that eventually will concern not one murder, but two. Whodunit? Was it someone within the narrow Condamine circle in Little Baring? Or someone who was farther afield, perhaps?

Moray Dalton mentions, in not an incidental way, a Condamine ancestor who came from Suffolk, recalling the author's own mother, who was born at Valley House at the village of Stratford St. Mary, and there is also a cute aside about contemporary American crime fiction of the Forties, which seems to be the lamentable Ozzie Condamine's favorite reading: "The sofa springs creaked under his weight as he settled himself more comfortably to follow the hair-raising escapes of a private dick who, on a diet of hamburgers and alcohol, made love to every woman he met while he bluffed his way through the jungle of American Big Business." A pretty keen-eyed assessment there! It is always fun to read the observations of classic British crime writers on the heady new stuff--some of it over 150 proof--that was then getting distilled in the U. S. of A.

The Condamine Case is another fine Moray Dalton detective novel, with true detection as well as interesting characters and compelling atmosphere. The film crew involvement adds a new wrinkle (I was reminded both of John and Emery Bonett's entertaining 1951 detective novel *A Banner for Pegasus* and the late M.C. Beaton's more recent *Death of a Scriptwriter*, 1999) and the supernatural legend aspect is superbly done. Parts of the book made it seem ahead of its time, like something out of a Swinging Sixties Ruth Rendell crime novel. I highly recommended it—but be sure to watch out for raven-tressed women who walk by night! Is witchcraft really dead in Little Baring? Test your mettle against that of intrepid Inspector Collier.

Curtis Evans

CHAPTER I
IN SEARCH OF A SUBJECT

STEPHEN Latimer's assistant director, Evan Hughes, the swarthy, sardonic, and fanatically devoted little Welshman who was always running his errands, when he was not hovering at his elbow with his notebook and his footrule and the battered Kodak camera with which he took such disconcertingly good shots of possible backgrounds, had collapsed just after taking the last out-of-doors shots of Latimer's second picture, *Blackpool Blues*. The trouble was acute appendicitis, and he was hustled off to the nearest cottage hospital. The operation was successful, but there were complications. The doctors and nurses fought for his life as doctors and nurses will for even the most trying of patients; and his idol remembered to send him bundles of newspapers with accounts of the triumphant London première of the picture he had helped to make.

Four months later he turned up one evening at Latimer's flat in Bloomsbury Square. Latimer opened the door.

"Bunny! At last. I've missed you. Where the hell have you been since they kicked you out of the hospital?"

"Convalescing with an aunt who runs a chicken farm at Manorbier."

"Where's that?" But he didn't wait for an answer. "You've come in the nick of time." He led the way into the living-room and switched off the radio. "Make yourself at home. You know where the drinks are kept."

"Thanks. I'll put on the kettle. I'd like a cup of tea."

"You old soak," said Latimer affectionately.

Evan, who was essentially a humble-minded person, was surprised and touched by his reception. He had not realized that he would be missed. "What about a meal?" he enquired. "Have you been out to dinner?"

"No. I couldn't be bothered. I thought I might open a tin of beans presently. I'm not hungry."

"I am. We'll have sardines on toast and an omelette." Evan was worried. Stephen looked tired and hollow-eyed and it was obvious that he had been smoking and possibly also drinking too much. He lay on the divan and talked while Evan prepared the meal and laid the table.

"The *Blackpool* picture was a wow. I've been compared to René Claire and Orson Welles. But a lot depends on the third effort. If you can pull off three you've something more than a flash in the pan. One thing, I do know my limitations. I can't do dialogue. Can't get away from clichés."

"What's it all about? Is it in production?"

"No."

Evan turned the toast and gently poked the sardines in the pan.

"How's that? Time's getting on. I thought—"

"I know. I've had several ideas, but never just what I wanted. There has to be a part to suit Stella Chance. Period, I think. I want drama with a touch of the macabre, and I'm keen to use backgrounds as Hardy used Egdon Heath, to get back to what some directors were trying to do when talkies came in and shifted the interest."

"How much time have you?"

Stephen winced. "Very little. But I'm going down to Somerset to-morrow. A chap I met has asked me down to his place. It seems there's an incident in his family history that I might be able to use. Condamine is the name." Stephen broke off to light another cigarette. "As a matter of fact, Mrs. Condamine is a sister of Doris Palmer's, those people I know at Hampstead. She comes up now and then to have teeth stopped and buy a new hat and so forth, but he very seldom shows up. He—it's rather a joke really—

he regards me with awe. Not a bad sort of blighter, but simple."

He went on talking, rather jerkily and disconnectedly, while they ate their supper. Evan was attentive; it was part of his job to be a good listener. His mind was the anvil on which Stephen hammered out his stuff. He wished he had not had to leave him so long. Stephen, like many brilliant people, was a fool about himself. He had hung about in London instead of taking a holiday and had let himself get stale. The process of hunting for and discarding subjects always got on his nerves, but if he had come to it after a real break he would have been more fit to cope with it.

It was past eleven before Stephen would let him go, though they were to make an early start.

"You are still in the same diggings round the corner?"

"Yes. There was a room vacant, luckily. Are you sure you want me to go down with you? These people have invited you, but—"

"You're coming," Stephen said. "I shall need you. I always do. And if the Condamines don't like you they'll damned well have to lump you."

"That will be pleasant for all concerned," said Evan, grinning. He did not really anticipate any difficulty. He did not consider himself a social asset, but he was very good at merging into the background, and that was usually all that was required of him when Stephen was about.

Stephen Latimer's appearance was undeniably striking. With his great height, his brilliant reddish-brown eyes, his mass of chestnut-coloured hair, he could hardly be over-looked or forgotten. His features were good, too: he had a short, straight nose, a mobile, sensitive mouth, a finely modelled if rather weak chin. Though his enemies, who said with a sneer that he was produced in glorious Techni-color, would not have believed it, he had little personal vanity. He used his charm at times deliberately, but it was always in the interests of his work.

"Nine sharp to-morrow, Bunny."

"I'll be ready."

They were going by car, in Stephen's ancient, battered, but still roadworthy Austin.

Stephen looked much less careworn in the light of morning and appeared to be in excellent spirits. The sun was shining when they started, but it clouded over as they reached Salisbury, and rain was falling as they emerged from the White Hart after a leisurely lunch.

Evan dozed, hypnotized by the steady swing of the wiper across the windscreen, and only roused himself when Stephen stopped the car and let down the window, leaning out to speak to an old labourer who was trudging home from work with a sack over his shoulders. "Is this Baring St. Mary? Which is the way to Little Baring? A quarter of a mile farther on? Thank you."

"What do you think of it?"

The two men had got out to stretch their legs and were looking curiously up and down the village street. Their informant had vanished into one of the cottages, and there was not another soul in sight. The only living thing was a black cat mewing piteously outside a closed door. A slow-moving stream overgrown with reeds and loosestrife bordered one side of the road, so that many of the cottages could only be approached by means of a rotting plank bridge. All were built of the local stone, had thatched roofs, and appeared to be in the last stages of neglect and decay.

Evan shrugged. "I wouldn't use it for a 'Back to the Land' poster."

"No. But it's perfect for period stuff. Nothing has changed here since—what's the date over that door? 1603. Well, we shall see. Let's get on."

They skirted an ivy-grown and crumbling wall and passed between stone gateposts crowned with rampant heraldic beasts holding shields, up a short avenue of beeches, and drew up before a portico with Ionic columns.

An old black-and-white spaniel which had been asleep on the steps came down to welcome them, wagging his tail. The door opened and his master came bustling out to greet them.

"Good of you to come, Mr. Latimer. This is an honour—"

Mr. Condamine was a stocky little man, somewhere in the late forties, with a florid complexion and child-like blue eyes that seemed to gaze on the world about him with mild surprise. He looked kind and faintly foolish. He was dressed in well-worn brown tweeds and leather leggings and his boots were muddy.

"Punch and I were out getting something for the pot. Rabbits, you know—" He looked at Evan.

"My assistant director and secretary," explained Latimer as they shook hands. "I hope you don't mind my bringing him along. I can't do without him."

"No. No, of course not. That's all right. Leave the car. Trask is about somewhere. He'll run it into the garage and take up your luggage. Come along and have some tea."

They followed him across a stone-paved hall. Evan noticed a big blue bowl full of hydrangeas on an oak refectory table strewn with an untidy litter of seed catalogues, dog-leads, cigarette-ends and old gloves. They entered a long, narrow room panelled in oak bleached by time to a pale silvery grey. There were chairs and a chesterfield covered with faded chintz. Everything in the room had been good, but was now old and threadbare.

A girl in a green woollen jumper and grey tweed skirt was wheeling a laden tea trolley over to the hearth, where a fire had been lit.

Another girl who had been kneeling on the hearthrug got up quickly and stood staring as if their arrival was unexpected. No, it isn't that, thought Evan. She has set a scene and we've messed it up in some way.

Mr. Condamine went forward fussily. "My dear, here's Mr. Latimer. He's brought his secretary. Mr. Hughes. My wife—"

Mrs. Condamine acknowledged this introduction with a hardly perceptible movement of her head, and shook hands unsmilingly with Stephen. She was a tall girl with a figure which in a few years' time would be Junoesque, a mane of black hair which was cut to shoulder length, and a face which Evan—who had taken a dislike to her—had to admit was photogenic. He summed her up as good to look at and bad to live with.

Mr. Condamine, who was obviously embarrassed by his wife's glacial reception of their guests, urged them to sit down.

"Tea. Tea before I take you up to your rooms, eh? Unless you'd like something stronger—"

"Tea will be very welcome," said Stephen.

Evan went over to the trolley where the girl in the green jumper was filling the cups. "Can I hand things round?"

Mr. Condamine intervened, "Lucy, my dear, forgive me. Forgetting my manners, eh? Mr. Latimer, Mr. Hughes. Miss Arden."

Stephen joined them. "If I may say so, what a charming name. I, too, shall hand things round. Are these potato cakes? I have a passion for potato cakes, inherited from my Irish grandmother."

Miss Arden, who was small, pale, and insignificant, smiled shyly and rather uneasily. Mrs. Condamine had, for the moment, been left quite outside their circle.

Evan, knowing his friend, realized that he had deliberately engineered this effect to teach his hostess not to be a toad. He was amused but apprehensive. Mrs. Condamine was probably unused to snubs and was, he thought, the type of woman who would think all the more of Stephen for standing up to her, and get her own back later on with Miss Arden, who seemed to occupy a subordinate position in the household and would be unable to defend herself.

But the group had dissolved almost before he could formulate his ideas, and Lucy Arden was left alone and a little apart with her tea trolley, while Stephen, having supplied Mrs. Condamine with tea and cake, sat down beside her on the chesterfield and turned to her with his famous crooked smile.

"Is it going to be a frightful nuisance to you if I decide to make a film here? I do hope you're going to be kind—"

Evan did not hear her reply, for he had to listen to Mr. Condamine, and he could not see her face, because it was hidden from him by a curtain of black hair. He settled down to the enjoyment of a solid West-Country tea, and had disposed of two potato cakes, several sandwiches and a saffron bun, and was just finishing his second cup, when Stephen, having lighted Mrs. Condamine's cigarette and his own, got up and stood with his back to the fire, dominating the room.

"I'm so sorry, Evan," he said pleasantly. "Mr. Condamine had offered to put me up for the night. You had not turned up then, and I, most inexcusably, neglected to wire last night and ask if I might bring you along. I have told Mrs. Condamine that we don't mind sharing a room."

Mrs. Condamine said sharply, "But why should you be uncomfortable? Why not an hotel in Wells for Mr. Hughes? He could run over there in your car in twenty minutes."

"I'm sorry," said Stephen again, "but I must remind you that we are to spend the evening listening to the family legend your husband thinks might make a good scenario. If I'm taken with it I shall probably want to sit up half the night talking it over with my assistant director. Of course we could both go to Wells. That might be the best plan." Mr. Condamine had been looking puzzled and unhappy, like a child whose companions are playing a game he does not understand. He had turned very red. "I don't quite— Ida, surely we have two or three spare rooms?"

"Oh dear," she said plaintively, "this makes me look such a rotten housekeeper. The fact is, darling, some of the mattresses have been sent to be re-covered and they haven't come back. So there is only the west room."

"Very well," said her husband. He was unexpectedly firm and had even achieved something like dignity. "The camp bed can be moved out of my dressing-room for Mr. Hughes. The west room is quite large enough for two. Lucy, will you go now and tell Mrs. Trask to see about it. Trask can help her if she can't manage alone."

Stephen protested that they were giving too much trouble. "We can go to Wells. Really—"

"Please," said Mr. Condamine very earnestly. "I should be so hurt, so ashamed. I do beg of you. I—I asked you here—"

"We'll stay then. It's very good of you. But, look here, no camp bed. Isn't there a sofa? Bunny doesn't take up much room—"

After some further discussion the sofa was agreed to as a compromise, and Lucy, who had lingered by the door, evidently anticipating some change in her instructions, was sent off to find blankets and pillows. Mrs. Condamine, meanwhile, had not uttered a word for some time and sat smoking her cigarette and looking into the fire, indifferent and aloof.

Or was she so indifferent? Evan wondered. He was sensitive to atmospheres, and it seemed to him that someone in that room was in a state of repressed fury. He glanced doubtfully at her. There might be more in that young woman than met the eye.

CHAPTER II
A WEED LIKE HAIR

IDA Condamine was still awake when the men came upstairs soon after the grandfather clock in the hall had struck twelve. She heard the murmur of their voices, subdued to avoid disturbing the sleeping household, and then the closing of the door of the west room and of her husband's room farther down the corridor.

A few minutes elapsed before the handle of her door was turned. George, of course. She breathed steadily and audibly, hoping that he would think she slept, and presently heard the door being shut. She smiled to herself as she imagined him tiptoeing away like a well-trained spaniel sent to heel.

The rain had stopped after sunset, and the moon, rising over Dancing Hill, was shining through her uncurtained window. She could see her red woollen frock that she had worn at dinner, trailing over the back of the chair. She had told George that she picked it up for a few shillings in the bargain basement at Selfridge's on her last visit to London, and when he admired the diamond clip at the neck she had laughed and said, "Woolworth's".

The dinner had been a modified success in spite of a bad beginning. She had been a fool to lose her temper.

They had asked her to join them in the library afterwards, but she had refused. It was bad enough sitting in the next room and hearing George's voice droning on and on. Was it or was it not a hopeful sign that there were so few interruptions? Was there really stuff for a film in that old tale of the eternal triangle, two women and one man, with its dark background of a cult forbidden and accursed? If Latimer decided to use it, would he offer her a part? It would have to be a leading part. She wasn't going to play second fiddle to that simpering little blonde idiot Stella Chance. Acting experience was not necessary in a film. In fact, you were better without it. Look at *Man of Arran* and *The Forgotten Village*. George wouldn't mind. He could be in it too; he could come on with the extras in the crowd that watched the witch drown. Latimer was good with crowds. She remembered the roar of the mob at Tyburn in his first picture, *Mariage à la Mode*. Would they use a dummy for the actual ducking? The tradition was that Hugh Condamine had ridden his horse into the pool, lifted her body out from where it lay floating face downwards among the reeds, and carried her off, and that her long black hair was so tangled in his spur that it had to be cut away before he could dismount.

If only the film could end there! But even Ida could see that this was unlikely.

She sighed, turned over, and went to sleep.

In the west room Evan Hughes sat cross-legged on the sofa in a nest of blankets, looking remarkably like an amiable and intelligent toad, while Stephen Latimer walked about, talking jerkily and waving his hands.

"It's better than I expected. In fact it's damned good," he proclaimed. "Strong meat, Bunny, but not too strong for an adult audience. I may as well admit that I never really meant to touch it. I came down to—well, I try to fulfil my promises when I'm weak enough to make any, which isn't often. It wouldn't have happened this time if you had been with me. But it really is right up my street. Don't you agree?"

He did not wait for an answer. "Period again, but a hundred years earlier than *Mariage à la Mode.* Condamine's given us the main structure of the drama. That can stand, I think."

Evan grunted. "You'll have to watch out for an anti-climax after the witch-hunt."

"I know. The sympathies of the audience will be with her. We'll call her Vashti. But we've got to make them feel for Delia Street. She is an heiress, she has been to Court and had plenty of eligible suitors, but she falls hopelessly in love with the son of the squire of Little Baring. She is the mistress of Great Baring, with a household of servants, with an elderly relative as housekeeper and duenna, and a young orphaned cousin to wind silks and comb her lap-dog and keep out of the way when she is not wanted. She throws the handkerchief, and Hugh Condamine, urged on by his father, picks it up. He is not in the least enamoured, but he is flattered by her notice, and, being quite a decent fellow, he is prepared to make her a reasonably good husband. He has a mistress, the daughter of an old crone who lives in a hovel in the woods, and who sells herb remedies and charms to the villagers, and it does not occur to him that he need give her up; but Delia, who is jealous and possessive, makes a scene when she discovers what is going on. They quarrel, and the quarrel is not made up until Hugh's father, who is naturally very anxious that the marriage which will repair the fortunes of the Condamines shall take place, intervenes. He rides over to Great Baring with a penitent message from Hugh and induces Delia to come back with him to dinner. There should be some women in the Condamine household, I think. A downtrodden mother, or plain, subfusc sister."

Evan nodded and suppressed a yawn.

"Wait a bit. We're going too fast. After the quarrel scene we have an inn parlour at Wells. Matthew Hopkins and his assistants are interviewing the local justices with a view to rounding up any witches in the neighbourhood. That ought to be a good bit. There should be two justices all for a bit of sport, and a third, more enlightened and humane, but afraid to say much in case he is suspected of dabbling in black magic himself. An inn servant comes in to say someone outside is asking to speak to Master Hopkins. Hopkins goes out and comes back rubbing his hands. Two notorious witches reported at Baring St. Mary."

"It might be a good idea to have the third justice look out of the window and see the informer leaving the inn," suggested Evan. "It might not be Delia after all. Leave a loophole. But Matthew Hopkins never operated outside the four counties of Norfolk, Suffolk, Huntingdon and Essex."

"And so what? Don't be pernickety. We ought to get increasing tension through these scenes and in the witch-hunt, with the villagers, worked on by Hopkins, who persuades them that all the bad harvests, the dying farm stock, and the sickly children can be caused by the spells of Vashti and her old mother, setting off with their pack of mongrel curs, the girl running into the cottage and bolting the door—"

"Ugly," said Evan briefly.

"I know. But some of it will be only indicated. That's where good direction comes in. I didn't muff the Tyburn stuff, did I?"

"No. You provided the authentic note of horror, the horrid scene—not planked down in front of the audience but reflected in the shocked or gloating faces of the onlookers." He yawned again. "Has it occurred to you, boss, that Mrs. Condamine is the right type for the gipsy? Pity she's so bored with the whole thing."

"Bored?" Stephen laughed. "Be your age, Bunny. You don't suppose Condamine would ever have thought there might be the makings of a film in his family archives if she hadn't put the idea into his head? He goes through the motions, but she pulls the strings. And of course she's all set to be Vashti as a first step on the road to Hollywood. But I don't think I shall offer her the part. I don't say she wouldn't be good, but she'd be difficult to handle. That young woman's dynamite."

"You're telling me," murmured Evan. He slid farther down among the blankets and closed his eyes. "Can't we call it a day?"

"All right. I'm sleepy too, now I come to think of it."

Her husband and their two guests were already in the dining-room when Ida Condamine went down to breakfast. She smiled impartially and rather distantly on them all as she sat down to pour out the coffee.

"Where's Lucy?" enquired Condamine as he dealt with sausages and bacon.

"She's gone over to Wells to get some things I forgot the other day. Those jam sponges are sold out as soon as the shop opens."

"Did she take the car?"

"No. She cycled."

"I must say you keep that kid on the run," said Condamine as he helped himself to mustard.

"Rubbish. You haven't forgotten that Aunt Julia and dear Ozzie are coming to tea."

"Blast. Can't you put them off? Latimer's time is valuable."

She looked directly at Latimer then. "You are going to make a film here?"

"Yes. I think so. I'm taking to-day to think it over, but it's practically certain. I hope we shan't be awfully in your way."

She smiled faintly. "I don't think so. I might even find it amusing. You'll shoot some of the scenes here?"

"I hope so. Mr. Condamine is taking us round this morning to see the church and what is left of Great Baring and a derelict cottage in Baring Woods, and, of course, the pool."

"You can't possibly do all that in one morning. George, have you forgotten that you have to go over to Bath to see Quinton and Rand about that lease?"

"That's all right, my dear," said Condamine cheerfully. "I put it off. But you're right. I doubt if we shall cover all the ground in the time. Better make an early start." He looked at Latimer, who nodded, smiling, and pushed back his chair.

"I'm ready if you are."

Evan, taken by surprise by this sudden burst of energy, hastily swallowed his last mouthful of toast and marmalade and rose from the table to follow the other two. As he did so he glanced at his hostess, but she was stooping to pick up the napkin that had slipped off her knees, and he did not see her face.

Not pleased, he thought. Condamine, on the other hand, was as delighted as a child setting off on a long-promised treat as he strode along between them swinging his stick, and with his spaniel Punch snuffling at his heels.

"We'll go first to Great Baring. I'm taking you across the valley by the bridle track—disused now, of course. The house has stood empty since it was partly destroyed by fire sixty years ago. It's still very imposing from the front. When you compare it with our house you'll realize that Delia, from the worldly point of view, was throwing herself away. A case of Queen Cophetua and the beggar boy. Though actually the Condamines were the older family. There are fifteenth-century Condamine brasses in the church. The first Street was a hanger-on—what the Americans call a yes-man—of Thomas Cromwell, and got his share of the plunder at the time of the dissolution of the monasteries."

The weather had improved. It was one of those still, grey days that are called fine by the easily pleased natives of the British Isles. They crossed the stream by a decaying plank bridge and followed a miry path through the water-meadows to the rising ground on the far side of the valley. They came to the entrance gates.

"Not bad, eh?" said Condamine, enjoying their amazement. "Reminds you of the lion gates at Hampton Court."

"They are magnificent," said Stephen. "We'll shoot something here, Bunny. Have you the keys, Mr. Condamine? I see they're locked."

Condamine chuckled. "We don't need any. The wall is broken down on both sides. Practically every cottage or barn that has been built or repaired in the last two hundred years comes from the wall of Great Baring Park."

"Two centuries. But wasn't the house occupied until the time of the fire?"

"There were caretakers, but they seldom stayed long. The place had a bad name. Supposed to be haunted. All rot, of course."

"Good," said Stephen heartily. "If the ghost is photogenic we might bring him or her in. Or isn't it visible?" Condamine did not answer. He was leading the way, climbing the overgrown heap of rubble that was all that remained of the park wall, and he may not have heard. They passed through a thicket of hawthorn and hazel and had their first view of the house facing them some way farther up the hillside. From that distance and that angle no one would have known that it was virtually a ruin. The great façade with its elaborate baroque ornamentation had not been discoloured and the glass in the triple row of stone-mullioned windows was unbroken. Only, as they approached, the paved terrace, ankle deep with the dead leaves of unnumbered years, showed that life had departed long ago.

"Our white elephant," said Condamine with a wave of the hand. "If it had been habitable we might have got rid of it now. These west-country mansions are being bought for schools. There wouldn't be any level ground for playing-fields, though."

Stephen looked at him quickly. "It belongs to you? I hadn't realized."

"All the Street property came to us through Delia. We were very comfortably off for a time, and then we slipped again."

Evan had been taking photographs with his little camera. He came back to them, his dark face alight with eagerness. "Look you, Stephen, this is beautiful. It is the proportions—" He broke off and said with an abrupt change of tone, "The dog. Where is the dog?"

"Punch?" Condamine laughed, but he looked uncomfortable. "He's nearly home by this time. He left us at the gates. He never will come in here; though, as you can see, the hillside is pitted with rabbit holes. Dogs are queer. They take fancies."

"I don't know that I blame him," said the Welshman slowly. "There's something about this place. A stillness. Is any part of it habitable?"

"The rooms in front on the ground floor might be. I used to come up here sometimes when I was a boy with my brother, when we dared each other, and we peeped in at the windows."

"What did you see?"

"The furniture was all removed at the time of the fire, but some of the curtains had been left and had rotted away. I remember once seeing a heap of faded rose-coloured brocade and torn paper in one corner by a hole in the wainscot, and rats running over it, and there were brass chandeliers hanging from the ceilings, green with verdigris and grey with spiders' webs."

"You never ventured in?"

"We hadn't the keys then, and we'd have been thrashed for coming near the place. Come round the side and see what happened at the back."

They crossed the terrace over the thick carpet of dead leaves. They saw then that by some freak of chance, possibly through some change in the wind, or through the roof falling in and smothering the flames, the front part of the mansion had been cut clean off like a piece of cake, while the rest of the building had crumbled into a huge mass of rubble which, in the course of time, had become overgrown with weeds. There were even some fair-sized trees, mountain ash and laburnum, that had sprung up among the broken stones and blackened mortar.

"Reminds you of some of the blitzed areas in London, doesn't it," said Condamine. "Do you want to stay here? Because if you do, I'll leave you to it, if you don't mind. It gives me the willies."

"No. We'll come with you," said Latimer. "It's very impressive, but I don't know if we can use it. I'll have to think it over. What have you found, Evan?"

Condamine was leading the way through a tangle of long grass and trailing briars which must once have been a rose garden, and Evan had turned aside to peer into a patch of rushes and iris.

"This must have been a goldfish pool. I can see a bit of the stone coping, and there's still water. There's an odd sort of weed growing under the surface. It looks exactly like black hair."

"I say, do you mind—" Condamine's voice sounded suddenly shrill. "We ought to be getting on. We—we shall be late for lunch—"

To their utter astonishment he broke into a clumsy, stumbling run. They both felt that they must keep up with him. When they stopped at the foot of the hill by the great wrought-iron gates Latimer was out of breath, and the little Welshman, who had not yet got over his recent illness, was rather white about the lips.

They both stared at Condamine, whose florid complexion had gone patchy and who was mopping his forehead.

"Sorry," he said disarmingly. "The fact is you gave me a turn. There's something you couldn't have known, for I never told you. Never mind now. I was going to take you home by way of the pool in which the girl was drowned, but I think we've done enough for one morning. I can see you're tired. You aren't used to trudging over rough ground, eh? We might have a look at the church this afternoon. I want you to meet the rector. I told him you were coming down and he was tremendously interested. It's an event for us, you know; something to talk about for years to come."

They were moving again, but at a more reasonable pace, and the other two realized that Condamine was becoming more his normal self. Soon he was telling them about his turkeys and his runner ducks. "We got top prices for them years ago. We kept cows when I was a boy. My mother was very proud of her dairy, but Ida can't be bothered with that sort of thing. I suppose you know a lot of the film-stars personally, Latimer?"

Stephen complied with a few anecdotes, rather as he might have indulged a small boy, while his assistant director trudged along behind them, silent and thoughtful. He was sensitive to atmosphere, and all the time they were exploring the shell of the great house he had been definitely uneasy. Then Condamine had undoubtedly received a shock. But what kind of a shock? They had been with him all the time and had neither seen nor heard anything to account for his strange behaviour. Evan rather liked his host, and there had been moments when he had felt sorry for him. There was something engaging in his mixture of diffidence and enthusiasm. It was evident that his mental age was still about fourteen—a fact that made it unlikely that he could cope successfully with his domestic problems.

They were just turning in at the gates of Little Baring when Lucy Arden came up, wheeling her bicycle. She looked pale and tired and explained that she had a puncture and had to walk the last two miles. Her carrier was full of parcels and so was the string bag hanging from her handlebars.

Condamine was sympathetic. "Too bad. You should have had the car."

"Ida said you were going to Bath."

"Oh, of course. She didn't know I was putting off my appointment. This film business is more important. Won't it be a thrill, Lucy, when we go to the cinema and see the places we know so well on the screen? By jove, I can hardly wait."

He walked on up the drive with Latimer.

Lucy had stopped to rearrange her parcels, which were threatening to fall out of the basket. Evan waited for her.

"I'm afraid you're not so keen on the prospective invasion?" he said.

She looked at him, then looked away. "Are you giving her a part?"

"I don't know. I don't think so."

"There will be trouble if you don't. She's—she's used to getting her own way."

"I dare say. But acting for films is darned hard work. Face and hair messed about, blinding lights. You hang around for hours, and then get shoved about and sworn at. How would she like that?"

She smiled at the picture he evoked, a brief, reluctant smile. "Not at all."

"Would you care to be in it?"

"Oh no," she exclaimed in tones of such heartfelt sincerity that he had to laugh.

"Splendid," he said. "It is a part of my secretarial duties to fend off film-struck females of all ages and sizes. Are you really completely uninterested?"

She did not answer at once. After a pause she said in rather a low voice. "I don't want my cousin to be worried—or hurt."

"Your cousin?"

"Mr. Condamine." She looked up at him anxiously. "Perhaps I have said too much. But I've noticed you don't talk much, and when you do you try to smooth things over. I believe I can trust you."

Evan, who liked to consider himself hard-boiled, was oddly touched by this tribute. There was no time for more. They parted in the hall, she going towards the servants' quarters while he went upstairs to get ready for lunch.

CHAPTER III
A TRIANGLE

LATIMER, who detested mud, not only changed his shoes and his slacks but took a leisurely bath, and came down ten minutes after the others had sat down to their lunch. This might have annoyed some hostesses, especially as the bath meant there would be no warm water for washing up, but Ida Condamine's moods were not dependent on domestic affairs, and, for the first time since the visitors arrived, she appeared to be in good spirits, smiling indulgently at her rosy-faced little husband and listening to Stephen's anecdotes about film-stars and more or less amusing incidents that had occurred during the taking of pictures without any signs of boredom or contempt. It was remarkable, thought Evan, how they all expanded under this milder regime. Evidently, in this household Ida's face was the barometer; when it was set fair the family came out and sunned themselves, when stormy they looked for cover.

They were not to visit the church that afternoon, after all. Condamine had heard the rector had to attend a meeting in Wells, but would be delighted to show Mr. Latimer and his assistant director anything they wished to see the next day any time after matins.

"On the other hand," said Condamine, "Ida says Quinton and Rand wired and are urgent about that matter of the lease, so I'm afraid I must run over to Bath. Ida says she will take you to the pool, or to the ruined cottage in Owl's Wood. We don't really know if the gipsy girl and her old mother lived there, but that's the tradition, and the village women and children give it a wide berth even when they are out blackberrying, though the berries on those bushes growing out of the crumbling walls are the finest I ever saw."

"We must start directly after lunch," his wife said. "We mustn't forget Julia and Ozzie are coming to tea. If I'm not here when they arrive she'll be even more unbearable than usual."

"She doesn't mean to be, darling," said Condamine, "and Ozzie is one of your most ardent admirers."

Evan noticed that she moved her shoulders, involuntarily he thought, as if shrugging off something distasteful. "We'll be off now. Lucy dear, you'll see about the best china and a lace-edged cloth and all the rest of it. Are you ready, Mr. Latimer?"

Stephen finished his coffee and pushed back his chair. "Right. I think you've walked enough for to-day, Bunny. You look tired. You might get on with the script. You know what I want. Pen portraits, character studies of the principals. Hugh and his father, Delia Street, and the girl Vashti."

"Very well," said Evan. He would not have cried off, but it was true that he was tired, and the pen pictures were a necessary part of the preliminary work Latimer always put into his pictures.

"Make any use you like of the library," said Condamine heartily. "You'll find ink and blotting-paper there. Look, Ida, I'll give you both a lift as far as the corner of Owl's Wood. It'll save you a mile."

The library was a pleasant room. There were not many books, and Evan had gathered from something their host let fall that those of any value had been sold. Condamine had bustled in before he left to pick out those that might be of some use from the shelves and dumped them on a chair.

"Here you are. Old account books and diaries. You'll find markers in the pages with relevant entries."

Evan thanked him. "But I must remind you, sir, that this isn't going to be a documentary. You must not expect Latimer to stick to facts if they don't suit him."

"Oh, he'll have a free hand, of course."

He hurried away, and a minute later Evan heard the clashing of gears as the car started. It was quite in character, he thought, that Condamine should be a clumsy, impulsive driver.

Evan settled down, with a sigh of satisfaction, to the work he most enjoyed. If circumstances had permitted, he would have liked to write novels. This was the next best thing. He could be as diffuse as he liked and build up the story with any number of scenes, some of which might be quite unactable. That would not matter. Latimer would pick out the material he could use from the mass. He could incorporate scraps of dialogue, questions of motive, descriptions of scenery, anything that seemed likely to bring the warmth and urgency of reality to the drama.

For a while he scribbled away with only an occasional pause for reflection. The house was very still, as houses in the heart of the country can be in late summer afternoons when the birds have ceased to sing. He hardly noticed the ticking of the grandfather clock in the hall, marking the passing of time, and the whirring of the lawn mower was too far away to disturb him. He was absorbed in the joy and the effort of creation. Lucy peeped in once to make sure he had everything he wanted, and seeing the rumpled dark head bent over the open exercise book, and hearing the busy scratching of his pen, went away again, smiling to herself.

Presently he became aware that the room seemed darker and realized that the sun had passed away from that side of the house. He got up to stretch his legs, and lit a cigarette. It was time to read over what he had written:

"Boy meets girl. Delia Street is an heiress and a fine lady and Hugh is the son of a yeoman farmer. The social inequalities would not matter when they were children. Opening scene Hugh and his sister Joan playing in a hay-field. Delia rides by on her pony, followed by a mounted manservant. The Condamine children call to her to join them and they play together. Shot of Delia riding home and entering Great Baring Park through the wrought-iron gates, looking back wistfully, a lonely little figure in her plumed hat and satin riding habit. Next shot the same field in early spring, with Hugh sowing seed (or doing some other agricultural chore). Delia rides by as before, but she is now a grown woman. (*Note.*—Must be over-age, or guardians would have stopped any romantic nonsense.) She beckons to Hugh, who comes up to the gate and they have a conversation.

"'You know who I am, Mr. Condamine?'

"'Of course. We heard you had come back to Great Baring. You'll find it dull here, ma'am, after the Court, and the routs and assemblies.'

"'I don't think so. I am tired of crowds and lights and noise and empty words. I think I shall like the country. Your family are well?'

"'My father is well. My mother died last year. My sister Joan keeps house for us.'

"'I am sorry you have lost your mother. I do not remember mine. Is Joan pretty?'

"'She's passable. Much as she was. She hasn't changed like you have.'

"'You think I've grown ugly?'

"'You know I didn't mean that.'

"'Well, some day perhaps you will tell me what you did mean. Now I must ride home to Great Baring or my good old Cousin Letitia will think I am lost; and you must get on with your sowing.'

"The next scene might be supper in the farm kitchen with Hugh telling his father and sister how Miss Street stopped to talk to him. I rather fancy a scene in church, with Miss Delia with her chaperon and a subfusc younger woman sitting in the Great Baring pew, raised like the royal box above the congregation in the nave, and catching the eye of Hugh in the humbler Condamine pew. (*Query.*— Would the rector allow us to take shots in the church if it proves to be a good background? Doubtful.)

"Delia is spoiled, arrogant, possessive; she has always had everything she wanted, and now she wants Hugh. Hugh quite sincerely admires the first fine lady he has ever seen at close quarters, and is naturally flattered by her notice. Vashti must come in here. Should she have been indicated before? A barefooted, ragged child peering through the hedge at the other three playing in the hay-field.

"The next shot might be Vashti coming up the village street and the village women picking up the children and turning away or running into their cottages and slamming the doors as she passes. Then her meeting—which should obviously be an assignation and not the first—with Hugh in the woods. No complexities or half-tones about Vashti. Hugh is her man, and that's all there is to it. *Vénus toute entière a sa proie attachée.* This is an A film, anyway. I don't think Vashti need utter a single word until the very end when she screams her lover's name as she is being forced down under the water. We'll see about that. She may have to speak to warn her mother the crowd are coming. . . .

"That takes care of the principals. Then there's Hugh's father. His point of view should emerge in that first scene at supper in the farm kitchen. The Streets have gone up in the world, but the Condamines were landowners before they were heard of. There was a Condamine at Agincourt. There's the brass and the tablets in the church.

"He will be gratified when Delia, using her elderly duenna as a go-between, indicates that she is prepared to give a favourable answer to a formal proposal for her hand, gratified but not overwhelmed. It is, of course, a great piece of luck, but no more than they deserve. 'My boy will make her a better husband than any of those Court gallants, and the Condamines can hold up their heads with any family in the country.'

"Hugh will be surprised but not unwilling. He likes Delia, and his father paints a rosy picture of their future: 'Horses to ride, and silk gowns, and maybe a chance for Joan to marry well, and a prize bull to improve the dairy strain. Lots of things we've wanted to do and haven't had the money.'

"So the matter is settled and the preparations for the wedding are in hand; but it never occurs to Hugh that he must give up his gipsy mistress and he is still meeting her in the woods.

"There might be two readings of Vashti's character. She might be pathetic and devoted; but if she is made too sympathetic it will be difficult to get any sympathy for Delia. As I see her she was not complex. Female flesh unillumined by mind may be divided into two categories. Those amorphous blondes of Auguste Renoir, so reminiscent of pink-silk sofa cushions and lumps of dough, would be placidly acquiescent in any emotional situation. Harmless creatures on the whole. Vashti would be as harmless as molten lava. The scenes in which she takes part must be brief and violent. The ecstasy of passion, and then, when she is hunted down and drowned, the ecstasy of terror."

Evan hesitated a moment before he added: "This part can't be offered to Mrs. Condamine. It is only for a professional actress. No husband would stand for it, not even one so obviously under his wife's thumb as Mr. C. Or am I prudish and old-fashioned?"

Lucy Arden came in again, and this time without taking any precautions not to disturb him.

"It's past four and they're not back, and Mrs. Luke Condamine and her son are coming up the avenue. I saw them from the landing window. Would you mind coming into the drawing-room now to talk to them and—and keep them interested? If she's at a loose end she's apt to—to poke about, and that annoys Ida."

"Of course." Evan slipped his notebook into his coat pocket and followed her out of the library. "You look all het up," he said sympathetically. Her face was flushed and there was a white smear of flour on one eyebrow.

"I've been making scones. This is Mrs. Trask's afternoon off. But everything's ready—" She opened the front door before the visitors could ting the bell. "Hallo, Cousin Julia. Hallo, Ozzie. This is Mr. Hughes, Mr. Latimer's assistant director. Mrs. Luke Condamine, Mr. Oswald Condamine—"

Mrs. Condamine was a thin, dark woman with glittering eyes and teeth and an emphatic voice and manner. She wore a good deal of semi-precious jewellery that swung and jingled with every movement, and she had a disconcerting habit of thrusting her face very close to that of the person to whom she was speaking. Her son did not resemble her. He was very fair, with a plump, pallid face, and seemed to be half asleep.

"So it's quite true!" cried Mrs. Luke. "How exciting! We could hardly believe it, could we, Ozzie? And will my brother-in-law actually be paid, Mr.—ah—Edwards, by the film company?"

"Naturally there will be some kind of financial arrangement," said Evan.

"How much?"

"I have no idea. That isn't my province." He remembered that Ida Condamine had described her sister-in-law as unbearable. He was inclined to agree with her. Mrs. Luke herded him before her into a corner with the skill of a sheepdog coping with a recalcitrant member of the flock. "One reads of such vast sums being paid for stories. *Gone with the Wind* and all that. Fancy poor old George pulling off a thing like that!" she exclaimed.

"You are thinking of Hollywood," said Evan. "English companies can't afford these magnificent gestures."

"Never mind," she said, laughing. "I shall find out. You can't keep anything from me. Where is George?"

"He had to go to Bath, I believe."

"Ida, then?"

Lucy came to the rescue. "She's showing Mr. Latimer round. He wants to take a lot of shots out of doors."

"Really? How extraordinary. I thought everything had to be built up in the studio, salt for snow, and a tank for the sea and all that, with arc-lights and everybody painted green—or is it yellow?"

Lucy had drawn her fire. Evan, feeling craven, edged away round the back of a divan, and, looking up, caught young Condamine observing his manoeuvre with evident amusement.

"My mother is rather overwhelming if you're not used to her," he remarked. "Over-vitalized or something." He yawned.

Ida Condamine came in, followed by Stephen. Evan, looking at them, was unable to decide if the expedition had been successful or not. Ida greeted her relations-in-law casually and introduced Stephen as Mr. Latimer, without any qualifications.

Mrs. Luke drew a long hissing breath. "*The* Mr. Latimer. It's such a thrill for us ordinary mortals to meet you like this. You must not mind my saying so. Marvellous, quite marvellous."

Ida Condamine glanced at Stephen and smiled rather maliciously. "You must not feel embarrassed, but I don't suppose you are really. You must have lots of fans. Oh, here's Lucy with the tea. Good, I'm ravenous. The more I eat the hungrier I get. It's awful. I shall be putting on weight."

Her sister-in-law gave her a sharp look. Evan noticed it and remembered it. It puzzled him at the time because it was in some way out of character, a measuring look, too cool and too shrewd to be in keeping with her, "Darling, would that matter? You'll always be lovely. Such an unusual type, isn't she, Mr. Latimer. But there I am saying the wrong thing again. Putting my foot in it. Please forgive me, everybody. Ozzie dear, pass the scones. Fancy digging up that old story about the witch-hunt. I suppose you realize they were all in it."

"All in what?" Stephen never hesitated to be rude to women who bored him. He was still being civil to Julia Condamine, so presumably she had been successful in gaining his interest.

"All witches. There was a lot of that sort of thing in those days, you know. It was so dull living in these remote villages. Baring St. Mary had its coven like the rest, and old Condamine, Hugh's father, was probably the Grand Master. Naturally when Matthew Hopkins and his assistants turned up in the neighbourhood they had to find a scapegoat, and the gipsy girl, being penniless and friendless, was an obvious choice."

"That's your version, Julia," said her sister-in-law. "George doesn't agree. There are only two witches in his story, aren't there, Mr. Latimer?"

"Only two," he agreed. "But it's a fascinating idea." He lit a cigarette. "There's something about this village even now, something slightly warped and uncanny, if you don't mind my saying so. All witches. Delightfully hair-raising, eh, Evan? But we can't use it."

"Why not?"

The room had grown darker while they lingered over their tea. The sky had clouded over and a fine rain was falling. Mrs. Luke Condamine's teeth and eyes and the crystals in her long ear-rings flashed in the gathering dusk. It occurred to Evan that she looked very like a witch herself. The others all sat very still. He was aware of Lucy Arden on his right breathing rather quickly.

Stephen was still good-humoured. He had reached the stage of creation when it helped him to discuss every phase of his subject.

"The White Queen could believe any number of things before breakfast, but the average film audience hasn't such a good digestion. We must be careful how much we give them to swallow. I want to concentrate on the haunting that wrecked the marriage of Hugh Condamine and Delia Street. To get the full effect of that they must be ordinary folk with no special knowledge of the occult, and, in fact, there won't be anything to suggest that the gipsy and her mother really were witches except in the eyes of the ignorant and superstitious villagers."

"A pity," said Julia Condamine. "You can see the hilltop on which the coven met for their sabbaths from this window. A cone-shaped hill like a smaller edition of Glastonbury Tor, but with five pine trees on the top instead of a tower. Dancing Hill. You'll find it on the ordnance map.

That's where—But George will have told you that—or if he hasn't that's his business."

No one made any comment on this. Evan sighed involuntarily. He felt tired and chilly. There was something unfriendly in the atmosphere of the room. Worse than that. He could feel hatred crawling there like an actual presence, like a venomous snake, an adder lying hidden, coiled, and ready to strike. Rubbish, he thought irritably.

He should have gone out again instead of working all the afternoon on the script.

The silence was broken by Ozzie Condamine. "Bound to be several interpretations of the few known facts," he said languidly. "As to what happened to Delia, for instance, and if she was a nasty piece of work or a victim. Pay your money and take your choice. I've a theory, but I'm keeping it to myself. And the actual truth was probably something else. Shall I put another log on the fire, Ida? This house never gets really warm. It didn't when we lived here, did it, Mother?"

Chapter IV
THE POWERS OP THE AIR

"WELL, what's the programme for to-morrow?" asked Condamine cheerfully. They had been playing bridge all the evening and he and Evan had held all the best cards. He was in high spirits, his florid, good-humoured face beaming at his wife across the table. Ida Condamine looked sulky. Her frock of flame-coloured velvet was very becoming if rather excessive for a quiet evening at home.

Latimer answered: "We must run up to Town, and I'd like to make an early start if that won't put you out, Mrs. Condamine."

"Not at all," she said coolly. "Why should it? Mrs. Trask or Lucy will get your breakfast at any time that suits you."

Condamine was looking like a disappointed child. "I say! Does that mean that you are turning the whole thing down? I'm sorry. I thought—"

"Not at all. It means that I have to see some of the people at the top and explain what I want to do. They'll carry on with the business side of the show and sending papers down for you to sign. Then I shall probably take Stella Chance out to dinner and talk it all over with her. I hope to get back here on Friday and get on with the script."

"I see, I see," said Condamine eagerly. "And when will you start taking the picture?"

"As soon as possible. But there's always a lot of donkey work. And look here, sir, we mustn't take advantage of your hospitality. Evan and I will stay in Wells."

"You'll do nothing of the sort. If you do, we really shall be offended, shan't we, Ida? You'll come back here. We'll get those darned mattresses back from the cleaner's and Mr. Hughes shall have a room to himself. Now, really, I insist." It was obviously difficult to refuse without hurting the little man's feelings, and Latimer yielded gracefully.

"All the same, I'd rather stay at some pub," Evan grumbled as they prepared for bed. "We shouldn't have to waste time over bridge when we ought to be mulling over the script."

"I know. But I couldn't get out of it. Did you make any notes this afternoon?"

"Yes. You'd better go through them."

Evan sat up among his blankets, smoking, and smothering yawns. He knew he would not be allowed to go to sleep just yet. The night was very still. He could hear rain dripping from the eaves and an owl hooting in a tree not far away. He thought of the great empty shell across the valley, of the wilderness that had once been a garden, and the lily pond choked with a weed that floated beneath the surface and looked like hair.

"I don't like the set-up here."

He had not meant to say it, but he felt impelled to speak. Latimer, who had been reading the little black-bound notebook with rapt interest, glanced round at his assistant. "Neither do I. But don't let it get you down. The story's a honey—or it will be when we've licked it into shape."

"You haven't offered the part of Vashti to Mrs. Condamine?" said Evan anxiously.

"No. But she's still hoping. The pity of it is that she looks the part; she's cut out for it if only she could behave herself. But you're right, Bunny, it would never do." Latimer sounded weary and impatient.

"I don't like Aunt Julia."

"No. But her witchcraft complex is intriguing. Coming back this afternoon through the Baring Woods we were able to look down on the village from a clearing. The cottages with their roofs of moss-grown rotting thatch looked like fungi."

"Do you like what I've written so far?"

"Yes. The scene in the inn parlour at Wells with Matthew Hopkins and the local justices ought to be good, and—you're quite right—the figure of the informer must be seen as a shadow on the blind or a reflection in a mirror, unrecognizable. We must keep his or her identity a secret from the audience. They may guess, but mustn't know until the end. That should keep the interest from flagging after the drowning of Vashti."

Evan grunted. "Vashti's is the best of the two women's parts. You'd better warn Stella that the gipsy will steal the picture if she doesn't put every ounce she's got into it."

"I will. But Stella is a good trouper. She isn't temperamental, thank God. Look here, Bunny, I've been thinking. I shan't really need you in London, and the time's so short. You'd better remain here to-morrow. You can give the church the once over and find out if the rector is likely to be helpful. If he would allow one or two shots to be taken inside the church it would save time and money —that is, of course, if it's photogenic. And get on with your notes. I'll be down as early as I can make it on Friday, Oh, and find out if we can hire a suitable field for a camp."

"How soon?"

"We'll say a fortnight from to-morrow. Mustn't start on a Friday, eh? I'll get through the casting to-morrow. I know who I want."

"Who will be Vashti?"

Latimer, who had been walking restlessly about the room with his hands in the pockets of his dressing-gown, stopped to kick an unoffending footstool.

"As to that—I haven't actually decided. Mary Lanyon did very well in that small part in *Mariage à la Mode*. But—I foresee rows, scenes, sulks—God! Why do I let myself in for these things?"

Evan said nothing.

Latimer took off his dressing-gown, got into bed and turned off the light.

"Anyhow," he said, "the picture comes first. Good night."

Evan had breakfast with his chief and saw him off in the car before he set off to see the church. He had not seen either of the Condamines. Latimer had told Lucy, who had appeared to preside over the coffee-pot, that he was leaving his secretary at Little Baring to get on with the script, and she had said that would be all right.

"Do you want anyone to show you round to-day?"

Evan assured her that he could find his way.

"I dare say you would rather poke about without Cousin George," she said. "He's a dear, but he's rather tactless. No need to tell him you aren't leaving."

"No. Not at all," mumbled Evan, and made his escape.

The church was on high ground, with a field, probably the glebe, between it and the nearest cottages. Looking up as he crossed the churchyard, where the grass grew long and rank among the sparse headstones, Evan was impressed by the height of the tower and by the extraordinary and menacing effect produced by the multitude of carved stone gargoyles thrusting forward from the roof like the garrison of a fortress preparing to repel all comers. He stood for some minutes gazing upwards at the horrid heads, grimacing, open-mouthed: giant lizards, pig snouts, figures from a nightmare, with scaly shoulders and outstretched sinewy necks and sharp talons gripping the eaves.

"Rather a sinister congregation, eh?" said a voice behind him. "The Powers of the Air."

Evan turned quickly. "The rector?"

"Sebastian Mallory, at your service. And you are the famous film director?"

"No. I'm not Latimer. My name is Hughes, I'm his secretary and assistant. I hope you approve of our enterprise, sir?"

"I am interested," said the rector.

They walked up the paved path to the west door together, the rector's silvery hair ruffled by the wind, his rusty black cassock flapping about his ankles as he drew

his companion's attention to the gaping jaws of the drag-
on's head projecting on the left of the porch.

"You'll find this sort of thing outside many Somerset
churches. I often wonder if the stonemasons were imported
or if they were local men. In any case they had a well-de-
veloped sense of the grotesque and the horrible. Inside the
church the roof is full of angels, all winged and some blowing trumpets—a glorious sight, I always think; but so few
of my parishioners ever raise their eyes higher than the
pulpit. Of course you see the symbolism. The gargoyles are
the forces of evil driven out of the Holy Place."

"Good," said Evan. The explanation appealed to his
dramatic sense.

"The interior is practically as it was when Delia Street
and Hugh Condamine were married here. There's the
Great Baring pew in the south aisle, facing the pulpit. It is
never used. Notice the carving on the pews, the pulpit and
the rood-screen. It isn't as fine as at Croscombe, but it is
genuine seventeenth-century work."

Evan sympathized with the rector's enthusiasm, but
the air of the church was cold and clammy and smelt of
mildew. He decided that it would be needless to ask Mr.
Mallory's permission to take a scene in the church. A
reproduction of the Great Baring pew could be built up
at the studios in a few hours, if necessary; but probably
Latimer would stage a meeting between Hugh and Delia
in the churchyard, an ill-fated meeting presided over by
the stone devils peering down on them from the eaves. A
chance for camera angles there.

The rector turned up the worn strip of coconut matting
in the nave to show him two very early and much-worn
brasses of fifteenth-century Condamines. "You see, as
I dare say Condamine has told you, they were the old

family, the original lords of the manor, and the Streets were rich *parvenus*."

"Is there a memorial to Hugh Condamine?"

"Certainly. In the chancel. Here you are—"

It had been an age of florid and fulsome epitaphs, but his family had found very little to say about Hugh.

HUGH EDWARD CONDAMINE
Born ye seventh day of June 1623
Dyed ye second day of November 1658
May he rest in peace.

The tablet, of yellowish marble, was oval and flanked by two small but bloated cherubs. Two lines had been added at a later date:

Also JANE, Relict of ye Above
Dyed ye tenth day of April 1662

Evan was puzzled. "I thought her name was Delia."

"Jane was his second wife. Nothing concerning Delia is recorded here."

The rector led the way out. In the porch he paused. "If you will come home with me I can offer you a glass of decent sherry. Is there anything more you wish to see here?"

"The marriage register for the sixteen-forties, if that isn't asking too much?"

"I'm sorry. It is. A good many of our registers are missing. The tradition is that they were destroyed accidentally in a fire that broke out in the vestry."

The rector was unmarried. An elderly and sour-faced housekeeper brought a decanter of sherry and two glasses into the shabby, book-lined study whose windows overlooked the churchyard, and left them. Evan was no judge of wine, but it seemed to him that the sherry tasted very like the liquid the aunt who brought him up used to buy from her grocer to flavour the tipsy cake for children's parties.

"Mr. Condamine thought you would help us," he remarked as he set down his glass.

"If I can, certainly." He hesitated. "I gather that he will be given a financial interest in the film?"

"Latimer has gone up to Town to-day partly to go into that. The Perivale Film Studios aren't a very rich company, but they have backers who are specially interested in the kind of picture Latimer is trying to produce, pictures in which background and atmosphere are important, as Egdon Heath is in *The Return of the Native*, and the moors in *Wuthering Heights*. I think they will be prepared to make Mr. Condamine a very fair offer for his story and permission to do as much as possible of the work on his land."

Mallory was filling his pipe. "Good. Condamine is badly off. His mother had a little money. But his father married again after her death; rather unwisely, I am afraid. There was another child, a boy, and very little provision could be made for him. He married very young and died a few months later. George Condamine gave his sister-in-law and her son a home. They lived with him until his marriage two years ago. Now they've got a cottage along the road. Ozzie gets jobs, but he does not keep them."

"Mrs. Luke," said Evan.

The rector smiled faintly. "You have met her?"

"They came to tea yesterday. I suppose they resented Mr. Condamine's marriage?"

"It is not for me to say. It would be a natural human reaction. But from what I have seen I should say that Julia Condamine tries to remain on good terms with Mrs. George. Condamine helps her as much as he can, but landowners seldom have much cash in hand."

"Oswald Condamine would be his heir?"

"So far. Yes," said the rector rather curtly, and changed the subject. "It is remarkable how traditions linger on in places like this. The places that are associated with the tragedy of Hugh Condamine and the women who loved him are still avoided by the villagers. Certain parts of Baring Woods, Great Baring house and its gardens, Owl's Wood and Dancing Hill. You'll never find the women and children blackberrying or gathering firewood there. I've no idea how much they know of the story; something, perhaps, handed down by word of mouth, but you would never get them to say. I've been here twenty years and I don't feel I know them much better than I did a few weeks after I arrived. They are a dying community. The young people go away and don't come back. Can you blame them? The cottages are undermined by the stream, crumbling away. There used to be a glove factory that gave them work, but since that closed down there is very little for them to do. God help them."

"We were wondering if they could be used for crowd work, but I'm afraid it would take too long to rehearse them," said Evan. "We shall be rather pressed for time. I expect we shall bring down some film extras in a couple of motor coaches for the witch-hunt and the scene at the pool—which I haven't seen yet, by the way."

The rector shook his head. "I doubt if you would get any of our people to take any part there even if you offered them special terms. I pass it sometimes when I visit one of the outlying farms. Just a sheet of still water fringed with reeds, a desolate spot even on a fine summer morning."

"The gipsy girl and the old woman were both drowned, weren't they?"

"So they say."

"Wasn't that supposed to prove that they weren't witches?"

"I believe so. A witch floated. So they were done for whatever happened, poor souls."

"Mrs. Luke Condamine has a theory that there was a numerous and flourishing community of witches here, and that the gipsy girl was their scapegoat."

"It's a possibility, but there's very little evidence," said Mallory. "In any case you wouldn't introduce a witches' coven into your picture, would you?"

Evan grinned. "Hardly. No. This is just my insatiable curiosity. I like picking up odds and ends of information as we go along. You'd be surprised, and not very edified, I'm afraid, sir, at what I learned about the night life of seventeenth-century London when we were doing *Mariage à la Mode*."

"I daresay," said the rector rather dryly. "But as to the story you are building up now, the material is three hundred years old, and much of it disputable. For instance, was it Delia Street, or some servant at her instigation, who brought Matthew Hopkins here? It may have been, and it may not. I shall be curious to see how you handle that point."

"What do you think yourself, sir?"

Mallory was silent for a moment. He did not seem to be aware that his pipe had gone out. "I don't know," he said at last. "It seems that she was very much in love. It is said that she was dining at Little Baring when a servant brought the news that Hopkins had arrived and had been haranguing the village people and had also brought a number of rough fellows with him from Wells, and that the witch-hunt was on. Hugh rushed out at once. The story is that Delia followed with old Condamine and that they watched the ghastly proceedings at the pool from a discreet distance at the edge of the wood. Well, that proves nothing. She might do that whether she were innocent or guilty of betraying her rival to her death. But what she saw then must have haunted her to the end of her days. I attribute that extraordinary obsession about hair to the effects of shock."

"Hair? I haven't heard about that. What's that?"

"Hasn't Condamine told you? After the witch business the marriage was hurried on and Hugh and his bride went off on their wedding trip. Hugh was trying to forget probably, and so was Delia. They seem to have been away for several weeks, or possibly months. When they returned Delia was greatly changed. Mrs. Balke, the elderly relative who had been her chaperon and had stayed on as housekeeper, and Jane Parlow, the young orphaned cousin to whom she had given a home, were both shocked by the difference in her appearance. Hugh was not blamed. The marriage seemed to be a tolerably happy one. But Delia was increasingly nervous, and kept a light burning in her room at night, which she had never done before." Mr. Mallory glanced at the clock, which had just struck the hour. "Dear me! It is one o'clock. I have been keeping you. You will be late for lunch, I fear."

Evan explained that as it had previously been arranged that he should go up to Town with Latimer and he had not informed the Condamines of the change of plan they would not expect to see him again until the following day, when Latimer would be returning.

The rector looked surprised. "But where will you stay to-night?"

"I shall catch a bus to Wells later in the day."

Mallory eyed him thoughtfully and said no more, but as Evan got up to go he asked him to stay to lunch. "I should be delighted if you will. I don't often have a guest."

"That's very kind of you, sir. Nothing I should like better. All this that you've been telling me is going to help us a lot in building up our story."

"We won't talk about it during lunch," said the rector. "My housekeeper is a local woman, and I don't know if Condamine wants the village informed of his plans. I have to go into Frome this afternoon, but there will be time for a pipe and a yarn in here after our meal."

The lunch, a rabbit stewed with onions and potatoes, followed by stewed plums with cream, was unexpectedly good and Evan enjoyed it. Afterwards they returned to the study and the rector resumed his narrative with evident gusto.

"On their return from their wedding trip Delia had had some sort of fit or convulsion as their coach waited for the park gates to be opened by the lodge-keeper, and had thrown herself into Hugh's arms and hidden her face on his shoulder. He had to carry her into the house, to the surprise and consternation of the servants assembled to welcome them home. They put it down to overfatigue after a long journey, but as the days passed it was only too clear that there was something very wrong. Then, one evening, when Hugh was in the dining-room waiting for her to come down to supper he heard a scream, a terrible cry that seemed to ring through the great house. He rushed upstairs, followed by Mrs. Balke and Jane, and found Delia lying on the floor in her bedroom in a dead faint. The mirror on her dressing-table was shattered. The women fussed over her, using the remedies that were the mode in those times, burnt feathers and cutting her stay laces, and after a while she regained consciousness and was put to bed, and Hugh sat by her and held her hand."

Mallory paused to relight his pipe and Evan took the opportunity to ask a question.

"Excuse me, sir, but how do you know all this?"

"My dear young man, there are letters and diaries. Hugh wrote frequently and at some length to his sister

Joan, who had married and was living at Winscombe, and some of the letters were kept. I am sure George Condamine would show you the papers he has sorted out from a mass of old correspondence in his muniment chest."

"Oh. As a matter of fact, he gave me some books to look through yesterday, but I was making some notes and I didn't get round to it."

"Perhaps my resume will do as well if you are pressed for time," Mallory said. "Much of the writing is almost illegible, some pages are stained with damp and some have been nibbled by mice. I deciphered them during long winter evenings when I had nothing better to do. George and I, that is. I often dined at Little Baring in those days, before his marriage. Just two old bachelors together—though, of course, he is much younger than I am."

"I see," said Evan, noting the implied though possibly unconscious criticism of Ida Condamine. "But do please go on. Delia had recovered from her fainting fit—"

"Hugh asked her what had happened. At first she would not answer directly but begged him to tell her if he saw anything strange about her. He said, only that she was very pale. She asked for a hand-mirror that she might look at herself and he brought her one and held the candle while she gazed at her own reflection.

"Hugh wrote all this down in a letter to his sister.

"After a while Delia laid the mirror down on the counterpane with a heavy sigh and said: 'Sometimes I fear I am going mad. And yet my mind is clear.'

"He said, 'What is it, Delia?'

"She said, 'You will not believe me.'

"'No matter,' he said, and then she told him that she had changed her dress for supper and had gone over to the dressing-table and was about to put on her ear-rings when she saw her reflection in the mirror. 'Hugh,' she said, 'my hair was long and black, streaming over my shoulders. Black, black as a pall.' He was, naturally, both shocked and bewildered. Delia was very fair and wore her flaxen ringlets bunched over her ears as was the fashion at that time. She had begun to cry and he tried to comfort her. I think it is clear from the letters and diaries that though he had never been romantically or passionately in love with his wife he was really very fond of her. He told her she was over-tired, overwrought. Of course there was some underlying cause. He seems to have put it down to the emotional disturbances that sometimes accompany the early months of pregnancy. 'When the child is born,' he wrote to his sister, 'she will have forgotten these whim-whams.' He had not heard the whole story, and you haven't either, Mr. Hughes, but I am afraid I must turn you out now and rush off myself or I shall not catch the bus to Frome."

CHAPTER V
OLD WIVES' TALES

"MR. DAVIES! Mr. Davies!"

Evan realized after a moment that the eldritch screech was addressed to him and stopped to allow Mrs. Luke Condamine to catch up with him. "My name," he said with deceptive mildness, "is Hughes."

"Oh dear, how silly of me," she panted. "I knew it was Welsh. The Welsh are so clever, musical and all, and I know you must be a great help to Mr. Latimer. I noticed you yesterday, so observant in your quiet way."

She fell into step beside him. "You are going my way. We can walk together. How did you get on with dear Mr. Mallory?"

"He was very kind and informative."

She tittered. "Really? But you must not rely too much on what—he's rather one-sided, if you know what I mean. I always feel that these parish priests living in remote country districts get warped and a little bit queer. It's the life they lead."

"He seemed quite normal to me," said Evan bluntly.

"Did he? I'm so glad." She stopped at the garden gate of a picturesque stone-built cottage with a thatched roof and mullioned windows. "Ozzie and I live in this hovel. Do come in and have a cup of tea with me."

Evan accepted the invitation and followed her up the path between a wilderness of overgrown gooseberry bushes and a neglected patch of grass strewn with wind-fallen apples from a gnarled old apple tree. He reflected that the plump Oswald might have got his weight down by keeping the garden in order.

"Ozzie is not at home," said his mother as she unlocked the door and preceded her guest into the tiny passage. "He's gone to see a picture at Weston. It's dull for a young man in a place like this."

"He hasn't got a job?"

"Not at the moment. He has great talent, Mr. Williams. What he needs is scope. Now if he was given the chance I am sure he could make his name as Mr. Latimer has done as a film director. I have been thinking that if Mr. Latimer could put in a word for him in the right quarter—sit down there, won't you. The kettle will be boiling in half a tick—"

He could hear her beads and bangles jingling as she bustled about in her little kitchen. Pathetic, he thought. And yet—there was an undercurrent of spite in her flow of talk. Now that he knew that until Condamine's marriage she and Oswald had been established at Little Baring he understood how much reason she had to dislike the younger woman who had ousted her. No doubt they lived rent free in this cottage, but it was a poor place in comparison with the Manor House.

It was an injury of which she must be reminded every time she looked up at the low-pitched ceiling and steep, ladder-like stairs and remembered the spacious proportions of the drawing-room which she had long regarded as her own.

"This is delightful," said Julia as she passed him his cup and proffered a plate of rock-cakes. He took one and found it very stale. She leaned forward, gazing at him intensely, eyes and teeth glittering in the dark little room so that he had to make a conscious effort not to draw back. "I do hope Mr. Latimer has realized how ideally suited dear Ida is to the part of the gipsy. I mean—she's so absolutely the type. It's such a chance for her."

"I don't think Mr. Condamine would like it," Evan said. "And I doubt if she would want it if she knew what she would have to endure. Latimer can be ruthless when he's trying to get the effects he wants. It's no picnic acting for him. The actress he casts for that part will be hunted within an inch of her life and half drowned in muddy water."

For a revealing instant Mrs. Luke looked very like a cat that has been at the cream. "But I think that's splendid. I mean—an artist has his integrity. Was Mr. Latimer taking her up to London?"

"No. Was there any question of it?"

"Nothing was said in my hearing, but I thought she might be glad of the chance to run up and see her sister."

"No. Latimer started early. I don't think Mrs. Condamine was up."

Mrs. Luke stirred her tea. "So often women marry for a home," she said thoughtfully, "and then discover that a home isn't really what they wanted."

"Mrs. Condamine is fortunate to have Miss Arden to take some of the burden of domestic duties off her shoulders," said Evan.

"Yes, indeed. Poor Lucy. I often wonder that she stays on, but I suppose she has her reasons. Ozzie always says Lucy is a dark horse. I must confess that I find her a complete enigma. One never knows what she really feels or thinks about anything. She's like an automaton. But I sometimes wonder if some day the smooth surface will crack and show what's underneath, and if we shall all be very much surprised."

"Human nature is a very complex thing," said Evan solemnly. It seemed the right moment to round off their conversation with a platitude. He was wondering, rather uncomfortably, what his hostess would find to say about him.

"What a nice cosy chat we're having. Do take another rock-cake, Mr. Griffiths. It is so nice to have a man of the world, someone really clever, to talk to. One is mentally starved here."

"Nothing more, thanks. Latimer and I were both very interested in your theory about the prevalence of witches here, though we can't make use of it. We only need one or two."

Julia Condamine laughed, this time with genuine amusement. "How funny that sounds. But of course you are right. You must edit the story to suit film audiences. If I had lived in those days I should certainly have belonged to the coven. To fly through the air, swooping across the valley on a wild autumn night when the clouds are like great black banners streaming in the wind. Lovely."

"But they didn't really fly."

"Didn't they?" Her eager voice sounded suddenly flat and tired.

An odd woman, he thought, as he got up to go, odd and unpredictable. If she was as queer as this when she kept house for her brother-in-law it was hardly surprising that poor George Condamine had decided on matrimony.

She went with him to the gate. He had told her he was catching the bus to Wells and would be returning the following day with Latimer.

"To stay?"

"I don't know. We may make Wells our headquarters. Mr. Condamine has been tremendously kind and hospitable but we don't want to impose on him, and once we get going things are apt to be rather hectic."

"George would love that. He'll be disappointed. But I dare say you are wise. I wouldn't sit on a barrel of gunpowder myself if I knew what it was. Good-bye, Mr. Williams."

He was still thinking of her as he sat in the crowded bus looking out of the window at woods and fields and grey stone villages, their outlines veiled in the gathering dusk.

She had made him acutely uncomfortable. What exactly did she imply?

In Wells he was able to book a room at the Royal Oak, and use their telephone to put through a trunk call to Latimer's flat. Latimer was in. He said he had had a satisfactory day and been allowed an extension of the time he would need to make the picture. He had rung up Stella Chance and she would be dining with him. He had told her she would have a great chance as Delia.

Evan agreed. "Even better than you think. I've got on to some new stuff. Look, Stephen, I'm staying to-night in Wells. Shall I book another room for you?"

There was a perceptible pause before Stephen's voice, coming thinly over the wires, replied, "Very well. Perhaps you're right. In fact I know you are. The Royal Oak? Meet me there for lunch to-morrow before we go on to Baring. Good-bye."

Evan strolled across the market square. The cathedral was closed at six, but it was only just after five. As he crossed the grass between the cathedral and the palace moat he saw a girl standing by the drawbridge feeding the swans. It was Lucy Arden, an insignificant little figure in a shabby raincoat and a black beret. He hardly knew why he went over to her, unless it was that Julia Condamine's comments had made him curious.

"I wonder if they are as cruel as they look," he said idly, watching the hard eyes and strong yellow beaks that offset the glory of the dazzlingly white plumage.

She threw a piece of bread to a cygnet that had been waiting hopefully at a respectful distance. "I am catching the next bus," she said. "Will you be back for supper?"

He explained that he would not be returning to Little Baring until the following afternoon.

She glanced at him, unsmilingly and said, "I see. All right."

He felt that he was being dismissed and was unreasonably annoyed. He was humble-minded where women were concerned, for they never took him seriously, but he could not remember having been actually disliked before. He said, "I hope I haven't done anything to offend you?"

"No. But, since you ask me, I wish you'd go right away. You and Mr. Latimer."

"Oh. Why?"

Lucy swallowed hard. Was she doing right? "I think you may end by upsetting everybody and doing a lot of harm."

"You mean by making a film at Baring?"

"By raking over the ashes of old fires, dragging ugly, half-forgotten, hidden things into the light. I hate all this prying into dead people's secrets. I always have. It isn't fair. Whatever they did they paid for. No good will come of it."

"It's an angle," he said thoughtfully. "Do Mr. and Mrs. Condamine know how you feel about it?"

"Of course not. It is nothing to do with me. And what I think is of no importance. But you asked me, so I've told you." After a moment she added, "And if you want to get me into trouble with Ida you have only to repeat to her what I have said."

"Do I seem to be that sort of person?"

She glanced at the lean, swarthy face with its mobile lips and deep-set brown eyes and said very firmly, "You may be. I don't know you at all."

"Well, that can be remedied," he said, and was surprised at himself. "You'll be seeing quite a lot of me in the immediate future."

"I suppose so," she said without enthusiasm. She had thrown her last crust and the swans were dispersing. She picked up her laden shopping basket. "I must be going now."

"Why do you stay at Little Baring?"

"I have no other home. I am very fond of George. Good-bye."

He stood by the edge of the moat and watched her pass out of sight under the arch of the gatehouse. Drab, insignificant, those adjectives still held good. But there was something about her, a steely quality, as of a sword in a shabby scabbard. She puzzled him. He was still thinking of her as he stood with the usual little group of sightseers waiting for the knights in armour to ride round the old clock as the hour was struck.

Latimer rang up the next morning while Evan was at breakfast in the hotel coffee-room. His plans were changed. He might be kept at the Studios. There was still a great deal to be done there. He had to see the dress designer and look over the sketches he would submit to him, and he wanted to interview some of the people who would be taking minor parts.

"Tell the Condamines how it is, will you? The lawyers will be sending him papers to sign. He won't quarrel with the terms. I've seen to it that they are more than adequate. If you can get any more material for the script, do so. I want Delia's part built up. Stella ought to be good in it. I've told her all about it, and she's very keen. Oh, and make a list of settings we can use and mark them on a chart or map. It's for old Sturt. He's to be our camera-man this time. He'll probably come down next week to study the lie of the land and work out some of the effects he hopes to get, but don't tell the Condamines that."

"I'm to stay on here?"

"Not indefinitely, of course. I want you. A couple of days ought to be enough. It's too early to book accommodation for the crowd extras. Can't be sure of the dates yet. I doubt if there will be any nearer than Weston. I thought sixty, and we might hire a few locally."

"Very well. Oh—about Vashti's part—if Mrs. Condamine should ask?"

"She won't—but, if she does, you know nothing. Good-bye."

Evan hung up the receiver and went back to his congealing bacon. Latimer was leaving him to hold the baby, but that was nothing new. It was a part of his job to clear up any misconceptions that might arise owing to Latimer's constitutional inability to say no as if he meant it. He knew that George Condamine had been allowed to believe that he would assist unofficially throughout the making of the picture, and that he would be disappointed.

And Evan wished he felt as certain as his chief seemed to be that Ida Condamine would not tackle him about her chance of an engagement. Why, he asked himself irritably, must a woman with a perfectly good home and husband hanker after a job that would involve her being painted yellow, chased through undergrowth, half drowned in a muddy pond, shouted at, bullied, and pushed around generally? He swallowed his last mouthful of toast and went out to see if he could hire a motor-cycle by the day. He was sick of the bus service.

Condamine was not far from the front door when he arrived, talking to Trask, who was digging up a flower-bed. He hurried over to speak to Evan.

"How's this? We didn't expect you until this afternoon. I understood that Latimer was to pick you up on his way down."

Evan explained. "It's like that in our job," he concluded. "Plans are worked out, and scrapped, and re-made. It's maddening at first, but one gets used to it. And actually Latimer has done all he can do here for the present. He's got the main idea."

Condamine looked crestfallen. "I see. I thought—I'd got the impression that I would be able to help—unofficially, of course, just standing by and putting in a word now and then, having the subject at my fingers' ends, as it were. Oh well"—he tried to laugh—"I dare say amateurs are a darned nuisance butting in, eh? And he's still going to make the film, isn't he? He hasn't changed his mind about that?"

Evan was able to reassure him on that point, and Condamine cheered up. He was like a child, easily cast down and as easily comforted. Evan explained that he wanted to work at the script in the library if he wouldn't be in the way, and that later on he might walk over to Dancing Hill, taking Baring Pool on his way.

"Shall I come with you, or would you rather I didn't?" asked Condamine humbly.

"I'd be very glad if you would come, sir."

"After lunch then."

Condamine left him at the library door after urging him to ring for anything he wanted.

Evan drew his chair up to the table and settled down to work. The rector had warned him that he would not find the old letters and diaries easy to decipher. They were even more difficult than he anticipated. Words and sometimes whole sentences scratched out, and others blotted and almost illegible; but at the end of three hours he had filled several pages of his notebook.

He drew a hand across his eyes, which had begun to ache with the strain. "Strange," he said aloud. "Strange. And horrible."

The door was opened and closed again. Someone had come in. He waited without turning his head.

"Mr. Latimer's stand-in."

It was Ida Condamine. She came and stood by him. "No. Don't get up." She was wearing a sweater of amber-coloured wool and a short brown tweed skirt. He knew enough about clothes to be aware that hers was a costly simplicity. "George says he isn't coming back. Is that true?"

"He's coming back, of course, eventually, Mrs. Condamine, but for the present he is more needed at the Studios. He's left me to finish here."

"Finish. What are you doing exactly?"

"This morning I've been reading some of Hugh Condamine's letters to his sister, and his diary, the parts that deal with Delia's obsession. Gosh! This is going to be some spine-chiller."

She frowned. "Do you mean after the gipsy was drowned?"

"Yes."

"She went mad, didn't she?"

"She seems to have suffered from a delusion," said Evan slowly. "You know what it was, don't you?"

"I've no idea. I'm not interested in Delia."

Evan realized that she was speaking the truth. She would never study any part but her own. For her the story ended when the water of Baring Pool closed over the head of the victim.

She turned her head abruptly as Ozzie Condamine crossed the terrace and disappeared from view. "They make themselves at home," she said irritably, "always dropping in for meals, and they think nothing of raiding the larder. I expect they've both walked over for lunch. You're staying, I suppose?"

If it was an invitation the phrasing was unfortunate. Evan thanked her and said he was not hungry and would rather remain in the library and go over his notes until Mr. Condamine was ready.

"George? Ready for what?" she said suspiciously.

"I'm going to have a look at Dancing Hill this afternoon, and he said he would come with me," he explained, wishing that she would leave him.

"I suppose that once George has signed the contract or whatever you call it he'll get the money?"

"He will be sent a cheque which he can pay into his account."

"How soon?"

"To-morrow or the next day probably."

She left the room as unceremoniously as she had entered it. Evan drew a long breath of relief and returned to his notes.

By degrees Delia had been persuaded to confide in her husband, and Hugh had written down some of her experiences in his diary, and had hinted at them in his letters to his sister Joan.

On their wedding journey, travelling by coach to London, they had put up for one night at the White Hart in Salisbury. She had run up to their room before supper to fetch her cloak, as they had planned to stroll out later to see the cathedral by moonlight. There was something dark lying on her pillow. At first she thought it was a black cat that had followed the chambermaid into the room, but as she went nearer she saw that it was a mass of black hair—or so she thought, for when she put out her hand to touch it there was nothing there. Some weeks passed before it happened again. There was evidently some curiosity among the former friends of Miss Street to see the country bumpkin who had captured the heiress, and in London they had numerous invitations to dine and sup and join parties to spend an evening at the playhouse or to go by water to the cherry gardens. They were supping at the house of a City alderman when Delia felt what she thought to be a spaniel nuzzling against her knee under the table. As she pushed it away it felt cold and wet as if it had just come out of the water, but when she bent down to look there was no dog there. Cold and wet and hairy.

"That's no use," murmured Evan, "unless she tells it. Can't be shown. There's the home-coming when she had some sort of fit as the gate was opened. He told his sister about that. What does he say?"

"She was tired and had been dozing during the last few miles with her head on my shoulder. She woke as the coachman pulled up the horses while old Reuben opened the gate and his wife and children ran out of the lodge to greet us. Delia was smiling, and then she looked up and her face changed and whitened and she cried out most pitifully and cast herself in my arms and clung to me trembling and hiding her eyes, and I could not understand it. But now she tells me that, chancing to look up at the stone griffins bearing the shield on the gatepost as the gate swung back on its hinges, she saw it partly overgrown, not by ivy but by long black tendrils of hair, some of which were loosened and streaming in the wind. Pray for us, Joan, for we are sore beset. We are encompassed by the forces of darkness. The servants have all left. They are afraid to stay under this roof. Mrs. Balke and young Jane remain, and the four of us are alone in this great house, with winter coming on and the long dark nights, and the wind crying in the chimneys and rattling at the window-panes as if there were something outside trying to come in. Delia does not leave her bed, and the women say she cannot be moved from this place until after her delivery. But I must not overburden your kind heart with our troubles. My service to your good husband. My father is, I believe, in good health. He has only paid us one visit, and that a short one, though this marriage, as you well know, was of his making. I look across the valley and see smoke rising from the chimneys and remember the old days when you and I were children and roasted apples on winter nights. God bless you, my dear sister.

"Your humble servant and loving brother,
                              "HUGH CONDAMINE."

"Poor devil!" thought Evan, seeing the luckless Hugh alone with his crazy wife and the two frightened women in that great desolate house across the valley. He remembered the weed he had noticed floating under the surface of the water in the lily pond and that it had reminded him of hair. A mere chance, of course, but Condamine had not liked it.

Lucy came in with a plate of sandwiches and a cup of coffee. "Here you are," she said as she set down the tray. "Ida said you didn't want any lunch, but you can eat these. I'm rather good at sandwiches." She sounded more friendly than usual. "I thought you just didn't want to be cross-examined by Cousin Julia."

"It's very good of you," he said gratefully. "I was hungry, as a matter of fact. These are tops."

"It's the flavouring. Just a suspicion of garlic, and the grated cheese is moistened with salad dressing. You are taking Cousin George out with you this afternoon. He was telling us. He's fearfully bucked. He's gone round to get out his car."

"I thought you disapproved of the whole thing."

"I do. But if it has to be, I want him to get as much fun out of it as possible."

Evan suppressed a smile. No one, hearing her, would guess that Condamine was at least thirty years her senior. But was he, in essentials? Lucy, he felt, was definitely adult, while Condamine was one of those people who never quite grow up.

"Why don't you come with us?"

"Me?" She looked startled at the suggestion. "Oh no. That would never do. Ida wouldn't like it. Besides, I'm busy. And I wouldn't care to climb Dancing Hill, anyway. I've been up it once, and once is enough."

"Is it so steep?"

"No steeper than Glastonbury Tor. There's a gorgeous view from the top, they say; but when I went up there was a mist, and the briars tore my skirt, and the Five Wardens looked—queer—looming through the fog."

"What are the Five Wardens?"

"The five pine trees on the top. I don't know why they are called that. Ozzie wanted to show me where the gibbet stood, but I wouldn't look."

"Oh. Was that where they—"

"Yes. That's why it's called Dancing Hill."

"I see. And you went with Ozzie. Of course, you're cousins."

"No, we're not," she said brusquely. "Not first or second. Something quite distant. That's George sounding his horn for you. You'd better go, hadn't you?"

Evan had to admit that Condamine was really helpful. They left the car two or three times to walk across fields to a viewpoint.

"You get a good light on the pool from here, with the woods beyond. I can imagine the wretched girl rushing down that slope when she breaks cover and being caught just over there, and when the ducking is nearly over Hugh would ride down over there on our left, scattering the crowd, and wade in through the rushes."

Evan realized that though Condamine knew nothing of the technical side of the business he had a natural eye for effective camera angles.

They came eventually to Dancing Hill, which was cone-shaped and showed some traces of prehistoric cultivation, though nothing grew on it now but turf cropped close by rabbits, except on the summit, where a shallow depression was filled with straggling thorn bushes and encircled by the five gaunt pine trees.

"A fine crop of blackberries there," said George, "but nobody ever picks them. Some view, eh? The line of the Mendips. There's the Tor. Sedgemoor is over there."

The afternoon, so far, had been fine, but the sun had gone behind a bank of clouds and a cold wind blew across the hilltop. Evan felt tired and depressed.

"We might take a few shots here. I don't know," he said doubtfully. "How does it fit into the story?"

"Well, the tradition is that this was the meeting-place for the witches' coven. I expect that's all bunk. What is fairly certain is that Delia's body was found here. Her child had been born dead and she was recovering. She slipped out of the house while the nurse's back was turned and made her way here. It would be about five miles by the field paths. When she was missed they made a search and eventually they found her. She seems to have died of heart failure. Over-exertion. It would be a fairly stiff climb for a sick woman."

"But—why?"

"I don't know. The allusions to his wife's death in Hugh's letters are very obscure. Julia's theory—I don't agree with her—Julia's theory is that the gipsy and her mother were innocent of any form of witchcraft and that the real members of the local coven came from Great and Little Baring, and that the Streets and the Condamines, being the two most influential families in the neighbour-hood, were able to divert suspicion from themselves when Matthew Hopkins arrived and provided a couple of scapegoats."

"That's not a very nice idea," said Evan mildly.

"I've always refused to believe it Hugh's diary was not meant for publication. I go by that. If Julia is right, they were monsters of hypocrisy. I think they were just ordinary people involved in something they didn't understand."

"Much more likely," Evan agreed. "I noticed you said just now that Delia's child died. You are not a direct descendant?"

"Not of hers. Hugh married again, you know. He married Jane."

"Oh, Jane." Evan stood gazing rather absently at the patchwork pattern of fields, pasture and stubble and newly turned earth. Jane, the poor relation, the humble unconsidered drudge. Jane, who might have provided still another version of the facts.

He had used another roll of film. Those pines against a moonlit sky with ragged black clouds driving before the wind. Yes, one could get some of the effects of Moussorgsky's *Night on the Bare Mountain* here, if Latimer chose to emphasize that angle. But of course Julia's theory was taboo. They must have some sympathetic characters. He turned up his coat collar.

"Chilly up here. Thank you, sir. I've seen all I need. Shall we get back to the car?"

CHAPTER VI
THE TIME IS SHORT

EVAN went straight from Waterloo to Latimer's flat. He found Chris Horton there with some designs he had made for the dresses. The table was littered with patterns of material. Latimer, who was talking to someone over the telephone, nodded to his secretary. He looked tired and dishevelled, but his eyes were bright.

"Glad you're back," he said curtly as he hung up the receiver. "Got some more stuff? Good. I'll hear it presently.

"All right, Chris. The green riding habit for Delia in the hay-field scene, and a hat with a yellow ostrich plume. I want a gay, spring-like effect: the rich heiress goes a-Maying. Hugh and his sister must be countrified.

"Chris has designed two sets, Evan. The farm kitchen and the parlour at the inn where Hopkins meets the justices, with a window opening on the courtyard where he interviews the informer. I think the audience must see their shadows on the blind. Was Delia the informer, Evan? Chris wants to know. That will mean another set of the yard."

Chris grinned. He was a gangling youth who gave the impression of having outgrown his clothes. His hair needed cutting and his nails were badly bitten and not overclean, which was a pity, as his long, delicate hands were his only beauty. He was one of Latimer's discoveries, and since he had designed the sets and the dresses for *Blackpool Blues* he had been hailed in more than one quarter as a genius. His ultimate destination was probably Hollywood, but for the time being he was under contract to the Perivale Studios.

"Your guess is as good as mine," said Evan.

"We'll play it that way, I think."

"She got her man," said Chris, sketching a girl's head on a sheet of blotting-paper. "Did they live happy ever after? Very nice, but I've been wondering if the end of this film isn't going to lack punch. The early scenes are good, I grant you, the witch-hunt ought to be a wow. The Chief wants the dining-room and a bedroom in Delia's house."

"That's what you asked for when you rang up last night, Bunny."

"The dining-room or the hall with the stairs," said Evan doubtfully. "You see, whether it was a guilty conscience, or the shock of seeing the other woman drowned, Delia never got over it. She was obsessed during the last months of her life. She saw things. At least it was always the same."

"What was it?"

"Hair."

Latimer, who was lighting a cigarette, looked up quickly. "How's that?"

"You remember Condamine told us when Hugh lifted the gipsy's body out of the water and laid her across his saddle her long black hair streamed down and was entangled in his spur. Delia and old Condamine were looking on from the other side of the pool. I suppose an alienist would explain it in terms of shock causing a recurring hallucination. She tried to keep it from Hugh, but had to tell him in the end. She was constantly seeing it, in dark corners, slipping off the backs of chairs, sliding off her pillow, a mass of black hair like a snake coiling after her. God! It must have been hell."

"Gorgeous!" said Latimer enthusiastically. "We'll have a third set for the Great Baring scenes, Chris. The great hall and the stairs. We'll have her running down them, young and gay and carefree, going out for a ride, before the hay-field scene. We're going to begin as we planned, Bunny, with shots of the mansion on the hillside and the farmhouse in the valley, and then a sequence in the hay-field with Hugh and his sister as children playing there and Delia riding by on her pony and stopping to talk to them, and the gipsy child watching all three through a gap in the hedge. Stein is sending up a bunch of kids for an audition to-morrow. You can attend to that, Bunny. Hair. Why didn't Condamine tell us that when he outlined the story? He must have seen I was worried about the end falling flat."

"I know. He doesn't like talking about it. He left me to find it out through old letters and diaries. The rector had mentioned it. Remember how he sheeted off after I happened to say that the weed in the lily pool looked like hair. It did, you know."

"Hold hard," said Latimer, "don't you get psychic. Restrain that Celtic imagination of yours."

Evan's face fell. "Aren't you going to use it?"

"Of course I'm going to use it. We'll wring every possible shudder and every atom of cauld grue out of it. How did she die?"

Evan repeated what Condamine had told him the previous day as they looked at the view from Dancing Hill. Latimer listened attentively but he shook his head. "That won't do. The hauntings must reach a climax. One evening at supper Hugh and the two women hear a scream. He rushes upstairs and they follow. As he enters, he sees something dark, like a rope, slide from Delia's throat as she lies in the bed, and slip to the ground. He can't find anything, but there's a bluish-purple mark on her neck and she's dead. And that will be the end."

"You could strike a more cheerful note, you know," said Evan. "He married again. He married Jane, the poor relation and domestic hanger-on, and they produced a family, and, presumably, lived happy ever after."

"Nice work if you can get it," said Latimer flippantly, "but a dreary anti-climax from our point of view."

"It's a great part for Miss Chance," said young Horton. He was an ardent admirer of Stella's.

They talked on eagerly. Occasionally both Latimer and Evan made notes, scribbling scraps of dialogue and stage directions. After a while Evan made coffee and cut slices of cake. Latimer seldom touched any but soft drink; and never troubled to lay in a supply of anything stronger for his visitors.

It was nearly one before Chris Horton shambled off, yawning abysmally, his shabby portfolio under his arm. They would be meeting again the next morning at the Perivale Studios.

The complicated machinery of film making had been set in motion, with Latimer at the controls. He would have no time, no thought for anything else now until the picture was finished. He had decided, with the approval of his backers, that he would play the part of Hugh himself. Why not? The director of *Citizen Kane* had taken the leading role. Olivier had directed and played the lead in *Henry V.* The Condamines of three hundred years ago would live again. Their descendants had become irrelevant and receded into the background of his mind. In the days that followed, days of frenzied activity, his assistant, hovering dutifully at his elbow, running his errands, was not to know if he ever thought of them, but at least they were never mentioned. No questions were asked, there was no reference, however slight, to Ida and her ambitions. Rosamund Harper, a young actress who had been a film extra in the execution scene in *Mariage à la Mode* and had been given a tiny part in *Blackpool Blues*, was to get her chance as Vashti. The unit was to go on location as soon as possible. The scenes on the set could be shot later.

After a great deal of telephoning, accommodation had been found for the whole cast in one of the hotels in Wells, though three or four of them would have to sleep out. A field had been hired from a farmer, one of Condamine's tenants, on the outskirts of the village of Baring St. Mary, and some of the technicians would camp there with the lorries that would convey the equipment. Victor Sturt, the camera-man, would come in his own car with a trailer, and keep an eye on his precious paraphernalia.

The cast had heard the outline of the story at a cocktail party at Stella Chance's flat, and they all seemed enthusiastic, though Ronald Burrell, the oldest member of the party, who was to play Hugh's father, shook his head over Latimer's determination to shoot the "witch drowning" scene at the pool with as few tricks as possible.

"This pond of yours may be deeper than you think, and it's sure to be muddy. Rosamund's a good kid, but, damn it, you're asking a lot."

"She won't be thrown in," Stephen said impatiently. "We can use a dummy for that. In fact, a dummy is being made. But I want a close-up when Hugh is lifting her out, and before that she's got to feel that she is actually being hunted, stumbling, breathless, exhausted. She must go through it on the spot. You don't mind, do you, darling?"

"Of course not," said Rosamund. "It's a simply marvellous scene, and I don't care if I'm torn to pieces. It will be worth it."

Latimer decided to go down to Wells, taking Evan with him, a day before the rest of the cast. The technical equipment would follow. There would have to be several rehearsals and Sturt would be visiting the proposed sites and considering camera angles before any shots could be taken.

They had lunch on the way and arrived at the hotel where rooms had been booked soon after three.

The porter took up their bags, but Latimer did not get out of the car. "I suppose," he said, "we'd better call on the Condamines. What a pest these social obligations are. Never have business dealings with friends, Bunny. It's a good rule."

"They were very kind and helpful," said Evan. He had seldom, if ever, spoken in such a tone to his idol, and Latimer glanced at him quickly.

"Did I sound ungrateful? I'm not really. George is a good sort. I like him. That's why"—he accelerated to get round a crowded bus on its way to Shepton Mallet—"oh, hell! He's had a sizeable cheque. I saw to that."

Evan said nothing.

It was not raining but the sky was overcast, and as they came down the valley into Baring St. Mary the string of thatched roofs looked almost too decayed for the word picturesque to be applicable. A dank marshy smell rose from the slow-moving stream that crept through a tangle of weeds and loosestrife. Under the little stone bridge two sniggering small boys were amusing themselves pushing a kitten into the water and letting it crawl out again.

"Stop a minute," said Evan between his teeth. Latimer, with his eyes on the road, had not noticed anything, but he put on the brakes.

Evan jumped out and ran back to the bridge. He came back in a minute carrying a tiny bundle of wet fur that mewed feebly in his arms. The two boys, after uttering one sharp yell of mingled fright and pain, had rushed blubbering into one of the cottages.

Latimer eyed the kitten with distaste. "Have we got to have that in the car?"

"Yes. I couldn't leave it with those little brutes." He slid into his seat and shut the door, and Latimer let in the clutch.

"Rather a pity," he said as he drove on. "The mother of those kids will be livid. We don't want to antagonize the village."

"Damn the village," said Evan curtly.

A gaunt black-clad figure riding an aged bicycle emerged from the Little Baring Manor gates as they were about to turn in. Latimer braked hard, and the cyclist jumped off his machine and came over to them.

"So sorry. I should have rung my bell, and I was going too fast. Oh, it's you, Mr. Hughes—"

"Glad to see you again, Mr. Mallory," said Evan. "This is my chief, Mr. Latimer."

The rector held out his hand and Latimer shook it and swallowed the acid comments he had been about to make on the reverend gentleman's lack of road sense. "I should have slowed down actually," he said.

"You must forgive me. Fact is, I'm on edge. I'm always like this, I'm afraid, while I'm making a picture. Hughes tells me you're going to allow us to take some shots of your church from the outside. If you see a suspicious-looking character in a torn sweater and a filthy pair of grey slacks prowling about among the graves, don't worry. That will be my camera-man. Victor Sturt. He's uncouth but a genius in his way. Well, we must be getting along—"

But the rector did not move back from the car window.

"You were going up to the house?"

"Yes."

"I hope you won't mind my saying that I don't advise it," said Mr. Mallory earnestly.

Latimer stared at him. "Really? Why not?"

"I take it you don't know what has happened? You haven't heard?"

"Heard what?"

"Mr. Condamine died yesterday."

"Good God!"

"He was only ill a few hours. They didn't realize how serious it was. When the doctor was sent for it was too late. He collapsed and was unconscious when he arrived. I heard it through my housekeeper who had it from the boy who brings the milk. A dreadful shock. He will be greatly missed."

Latimer seemed quite stunned by the news. Evan, glancing at him, saw that he had turned very white. He leaned forward to distract the rector's attention and said: "I should think everyone liked him. It's a shock to us too, sir. He was so pleased and excited—like a child almost."

"Yes. He had a kind of—of simplicity that was very endearing, poor fellow." The rector cleared his throat. "You have come down to start work on the picture?"

"Yes."

"I would suggest that you suspend your activities until after the funeral, as a mark of respect."

Evan had expected Latimer to acquiesce as a matter of course, and he was unpleasantly surprised when he answered unwillingly: "Is that really necessary?"

"I think so," said the rector stiffly.

"Very well. Please don't think me unfeeling, but our time is short and delays are expensive. I'm not one of those directors who are given unlimited financial backing." He added under his breath: "Not yet."

"It will only be two days. The funeral will be on Friday at twelve. Good afternoon." He mounted his bicycle and rode away in the direction of the village.

Latimer sat back and lit a cigarette. "A bad business, Bunny," he said sombrely. "I only hope—" He did not finish the sentence.

Evan said nothing. He was thinking of Lucy.

"We must send a wreath. See about it when we get back to the hotel, and get in touch with Sturt and warn him to keep out of the way until the—until it's over." He threw his half-smoked cigarette out of the window and began to back the car.

Evan opened his mouth to speak and thought better of it. He looked down at the kitten on his lap, curled up and fast asleep. Why were they letting this get them down? Everyone had to die sooner or later, and Condamine was almost a stranger. He thought: "I hope we're not in for a run of bad luck."

Latimer was silent, brooding, on their way back. There was very little traffic on the roads. As he drove the car into the hotel yard he said: "Bring your typewriter to my room when you've made those calls. We can work some more on the script."

CHAPTER VII
THE CAUSE OF DEATH

LATIMER did not come down to breakfast, and his assistant director sat alone at their table in the window of the coffee-room. They had been working on the script until past three o'clock, Latimer dictating while Evan took notes. He had stopped at last abruptly. "That's enough. I shall take some of my sleeping stuff. Tell them not to disturb me in the morning. We'll meet at lunch. Sturt will be here in the afternoon and we'll go through all this with him."

Evan spread marmalade on his toast and read the *Telegraph* propped against his teapot. It was pleasant to loiter for a change. He sighed when the old waiter came over to tell him he was wanted on the telephone. It would be someone from the Studios wanting to know why production was being held up for two days. He picked up the receiver impatiently, but his face changed as he heard the voice that came over the wires.

"Mr. Hughes. Is that you? Lucy Arden speaking. I—I think you're kind. Will you do something for me?"

"Yes. Of course. Anything I can. Where are you?" He remembered that Little Baring was not on the telephone.

"In the village post office. I came down on my bicycle. I have to go back now. Will you come at once? It's about Punch. I want you to take him, please, until I can arrange something. It—it's urgent. At once—"

"Very well. But—I say—" It was no use, the line had gone dead. He glanced at his watch. There was a bus every two hours that passed through Baring St. Mary, and it left the Market Square at the hour. He had just three minutes if he was to catch it.

The weather had changed for the better. It was a still golden autumn morning, and the stream running through the village reflected blue sky as well as thatched roofs and crooked chimneys. The woman who kept the post office and general shop was standing at her door and wished him good morning as he passed.

He had not realized that the avenue leading up to the house was so long. He checked an inclination to break into a run. At once, she had said, but she probably had not meant him to take that literally. The truth was that while he was vaguely alarmed he was also extremely flattered by her appeal. At the Studios people often came to him for help or advice or to tell him their troubles, but that, he thought, was simply because he had the great man's ear. Through him they could—or thought they could—get at Latimer. But this—he knew it instinctively—was different: this call was not to the assistant director but to the man.

The avenue was longer than he remembered it, and the house itself larger and more intimidating. He missed the moral support of Latimer, who was perfectly at his ease everywhere and in any company. Had she really meant him to come marching up like this to the front door? He knocked and waited, setting his teeth. He heard raised voices inside the house, and the door was opened by Ida Condamine. Her dark and vivid face had a welcoming look that vanished as she saw who it was.

"Mr. Hughes. What is it? Have you a message for me?"

"Not exactly. Of course—deepest sympathy—" he stammered.

"Oh. Thanks very much. You won't expect me to ask you in. It's hardly the moment for social calls, is it?" She seemed about to shut the door in his face, leaving him standing outside, but Lucy Arden came quickly out of the room on the left.

"Mr. Hughes has come to see me, Cousin Ida."

"You?"

"Yes. Please come in, Mr. Hughes. You're just in time."

Ida glanced from one to the other. She was no longer annoyed, but seemed to be secretly amused. "Very well. This way—"

Evan followed them into the breakfast-room.

Mrs. Luke Condamine was there sitting by the window. She was wearing the black dress she had bought in Bath the previous day. Long jet ear-rings dangled against her thin neck, and her bony fingers played nervously with a string of jet and crystal beads. Her sallow face was flushed and her rather prominent eyes strained and anxious. She hardly noticed Evan as he came in; her whole attention was concentrated on her son who stood on the hearth-rug with his back to the fireplace surveying the others, with an unpleasant half-smile on his fat face.

"Well, I take it that's settled," he said, ignoring the new-comer and addressing Ida. "I'll be getting along now. Mother can stay here and keep you company until after lunch. She can come home then. It will all be over."

"No," said Lucy.

"Shut up!" said Ozzie with a savage emphasis that contrasted strangely with his usual sleepy drawl. His mother started perceptibly, but Ida only laughed.

"Quite the he-man. Not very polite, but I'm afraid I agree with him, Lucy. I can't imagine what Mr. Hughes must think of this bickering."

"I don't know what it is all about," said Evan. "Perhaps someone would explain."

"Of course. It's quite simple. My poor husband's spaniel, Punch, is fretting for his master as dogs will. He would not touch his food yesterday, and he kept me awake most of the night whimpering and whining. George's death was a great shock to me, Mr. Hughes, and my nerves are in a bad state. I decided that the vet must come and take Punch away and put him to sleep. It seemed the kindest thing for the dog, too. I was talking it over with Oswald and he pointed out that the vet would be at Taunton as this is market day, and he offered to take the whole thing out of my hands and save quite unnecessary bother and expense."

Evan looked at the fat youth. "You have offered to destroy the dog yourself?"

"Precisely."

"No," said Lucy. She added in a high brittle voice, "He likes hurting things. They talk about it in the village."

For a moment no one spoke. It was the sort of silence that follows the crash of shattered glass. Then Mrs. Luke cried out, "Malicious gossip! Libellous! I'll never forgive you for this, Lucy Arden."

They all ignored her. Evan turned to Ida Condamine. "Perhaps you'll let me take the dog. I'll keep him for a few days, and if he doesn't settle down I'll take him to a reliable vet and see to it that his end is painless. That's what Mr. Condamine would have wished, I think."

"That's really very good of you," she said graciously. "He's chained up in his kennel in the yard at present. I'm sure poor Ozzie will be grateful to be spared a very disagreeable job. Actually he's very tender-hearted, aren't you, darling? You must not take Lucy too seriously, Mr. Hughes. If she doesn't take care, people will be calling her neurotic. You had better hand Punch over to his new owner, Lucy, since you have busied yourself in this matter. Goodbye, Mr. Hughes, for the present."

"Well, that was a pretty good covering-up job," said Evan as he and Lucy crossed the yard.

"Yes," she said. "But it's true, unfortunately, about Ozzie. Ida must know. I hate him. He's quiet usually, but since George—since this happened he's been excited. He and his mother will be leaving the cottage, I suppose, and coming back here."

Punch came out of his kennel when he heard her voice and jumped up at her, whimpering with pleasure and trying to lick her hands.

"He's fretting for Cousin George," she said, "but I think he'll get over it if he isn't neglected. He's used to notice. He followed George about wherever he went. Ida doesn't care for dogs. I hope you won't find him a bother. I'll take him as soon as I can make arrangements."

"You won't be staying on here?"

"Oh no. I shall be all right. George will have left me something. He said he would."

"And you aren't happy here, are you?"

"No." She unhooked the chain from Punch's collar and attached a lead. "I suppose you have heard there is to be an inquest. The doctor was not satisfied. He's a locum and rather young. I suppose he hasn't had much experience and isn't very sure of himself. They came yesterday afternoon with an ambulance and fetched the—and fetched George away. I was alone in the house. Ida and Cousin Julia had gone over to Bath to get mourning."

"What about the funeral?"

"That will be to-morrow just the same. Are you coming?"

"I think so. The Studios are sending a wreath, and there will be one from Latimer and me. I—I liked him very much," said Evan earnestly.

"He liked you. He told me so. He was so looking forward to the picture being made and seeing it on the screen—and now he never will—" Her eyes filled with tears but she blinked them away. "Please take Punch now. I've got lots to do."

"If you stay here much longer, Mr. Hughes, look you, we shall be starting a menagerie," said the landlady of the Royal Oak when he led Punch into her office. She was a stout, comfortable person, a fellow countrywoman from Glamorgan, and from the moment of their arrival she had allowed him to feel that he was privileged. "Our old cat has taken to that kitty you brought in, you'll be pleased to hear. She's got it in her basket with her own litter and licked it all over. But what's this?" She laid down her pen and adjusted her spectacles as Punch laid a paw on her knee and looked up into her face. "This is poor Mr. Condamine's dog. How did you come by him?"

Evan explained, but without any reference to Oswald.

"You can keep him here and welcome," she said, "so long as he doesn't disturb the other guests. Mr. Condamine was a real gentleman. He often came in here for a glass of beer, always friendly and nice. I don't know much about the rest of the family. It doesn't do to believe all you hear. You've heard there's to be an inquest?"

"Miss Arden told me."

She lowered her voice mysteriously. "Between you and me, Mr. Hughes, it's being held under this very roof. At least, not that exactly, but in the room built out at the back that we let out for concerts and socials. At ten o'clock, and I daresay it won't last more than a few minutes. Just formal evidence, as they say. They're keeping it quiet, but the public has the right to be there, and you can slip in if you like. The entrance is from the lane at the back, but you can get in by following the passage past the kitchen. It might be useful to you in your job. We had a gentleman here who wrote books, and he was all for gaining experience. But here I am with bills to make out and lunch will be served in half an hour."

Evan took the hint and left her.

He found Latimer and the camera-man in the lounge sipping cocktails. Latimer greeted him impatiently. "Where on earth have you been?"

"You said I could have the morning off."

"I must have been drunk. What have you brought that animal in here for, for God's sake? Don't tell me you've landed yourself with a dog just now. That really would be the last straw."

"Would it?" said Evan in his most wooden manner. "He belonged to George Condamine. He seemed to be rather in their way at Little Baring, so I offered to take him off their hands."

"Oh." Latimer seemed taken back. "In that case, of course—so that's where you went? Rather extraordinary, I must say. You hardly know them."

"Miss Arden rang me up."

"Really? Curiouser and curiouser," said Latimer with an attempt at lightness. "Sorry if I bit your head off, old boy. This delay just now is getting me down."

"That's all right," mumbled Evan. Latimer was always irritable and touchy during the making of a picture. Everybody at the Studios knew it and made allowances.

"Poor Bunny. I give you hell, don't I." Latimer was smiling now and his voice was warm and friendly. "You're looking rather under the weather. I tell you what. I'll give you a few days off. The unit should be here and we'll start work in earnest on Monday. Until then mooch around, please yourself. Sturt and I are going over some of the ground this afternoon. Rosamund arrives this evening and we may put her through some of her scenes up in the woods to-morrow. We shall keep well out of the way of the village, of course."

"You won't need me?"

"Not really."

"You'll not be going to the funeral then?"

"No. I think it would be rather intrusive. Actually I hardly know the family. You might see the flowers get there."

"I will."

The gong sounded for lunch and they went downstairs together.

During the meal, Latimer and the camera-man discussed technicalities. Evan said very little. Afterwards he saw them start off in the car before he took Punch for a walk by the field path to Wookey.

He was puzzled and uneasy. Why had he been left behind? He knew the ground better than Latimer, and normally he would have been needed to make the inevitable alterations in the script. Victor Sturt would reject some shots and suggest others, and his views must be listened to, for he was one of the ablest men in his profession. Was—Evan tried to face it—was Latimer getting tired of his assistant director? Was he beginning to resent Evan's lack of deference, his occasional criticisms? During lunch Evan had been ready enough to take part in the conversation, but he had been rather pointedly kept out of it. Evan tried not to feel hurt, and almost succeeded.

He caught a bus to Weston, dined there and went to a cinema where Punch was admitted as a special favour, and went back to Wells on the last bus. He found Latimer in the public bar playing darts with some of the locals and apparently in high spirits. They went up to their rooms together.

"I may not see you in the morning, Bunny. Sturt and I are going over to Bath to meet Rosamund and bring her along, and we shall be making an early start. Sturt's very keen. He says that wood is ideal for the sort of shots we've visualised. Plenty of briars for her to struggle through. I mean the sequence of Vashti being hunted down to lick what Griffiths did years ago with the big scene in *Broken Blossoms*. Lillian Gish, wasn't it, screaming in that cupboard? Good night, old chap."

"Good night, Stephen."

Evan had told himself that he would not attend the inquest, but when the coroner walked into the room that was being used as a court just as the clocks were striking ten he was there sitting unnoticed in a dark corner where he was screened from observation by a stack of folding chairs. The coroner sat at the end of a long trestle table like a chairman at a board meeting, with the jury on his left hand and facing the room. There were several men sitting in groups in the first three rows of chairs. No member of the Condamine family was present. The coroner, an elderly man, made a very brief opening speech.

"We are here to enquire into the circumstances attending the death of George Eustace Hugh Condamine, of Little Baring Manor in the parish of Baring St. Mary in this county. We shall take first evidence of identification. I call Mr. Jethro Rand."

A short wizened grey-haired man stood up, took the oath in a dry matter-of-fact voice and went on to say that he was a member of the firm of Rand, Quinton and Rand of the Circus, Bath, legal advisers of the deceased. He had been asked to view the remains and identified the—ah— body as being that of his client, who was also, he might add, a friend of long standing. He had seen Mr. Condamine quite recently, when he came over to Bath and made a new will. At that time he appeared to be in his usual health.

"Quite so," said the coroner repressively. "That will be all for the moment."

Mr. Rand resumed his seat and Dr. Fosdyke was called. Dr. Fosdyke was young and seemed nervous. When he had been sworn he stood fingering his tie. He was acting as locum for Dr. Lemon while the latter took a holiday. He had received a telephone call from Baring St. Mary at five o'clock on Monday morning asking him to go at once to Little Baring. It was an urgent call. He understood that the patient—Mr. Condamine—had been ill all night. The symptoms, as described to him, suggested a case of food poisoning, or possibly the breaking of a duodenal ulcer. He got there as quickly as he could, but when he arrived the patient was in a state of collapse and he died without recovering consciousness. He was not satisfied, but said nothing to the relatives at the time. During the day he thought the matter over and the following morning he decided that he could not sign a death certificate. He got into touch with the authorities who arranged for a postmortem which was carried out by him with the assistance of Dr. Campbell, the police surgeon.

The coroner took off his spectacles and wiped them. "And what were your findings?"

"Do you want details?"

"Not at this stage."

"Very well. We found unmistakable traces of arsenic."

"Enough to cause death?"

"Oh, definitely."

There was a murmur, quickly silenced as the coroner spoke.

"I shall ask no further questions now. The inquest is adjourned pending further investigation into the facts." He rose, gathering up his papers, and the court rose with him.

Evan slipped out quickly by the door he had come in. Mrs. Price met him in the hotel lobby. "Soon over," she said comfortably. "I suppose it was some internal trouble, poor gentleman. The wreaths have come, look you, and the car you ordered is at the door, but you've time for a glass of something before you start. You're looking rather pale."

Evan declined the well-meant suggestion and got into the car, sitting by the driver. Most of the room at the back was occupied by two immense floral tributes that would inevitably overwhelm those sent by George Condamine's friends and neighbours. Vulgar ostentation, thought Evan bitterly.

There was quite a long row of cars in the muddy lane that led to the church. The first part of the service was over and the coffin was being carried by four of Condamine's tenants, stumbling over forgotten mounds in the long wet grass to the open grave. Ida Condamine followed, in deep mourning, leaning on the arm of her husband's nephew, and Mrs. Luke came behind with Lucy Arden. There were a number of other people present, grouped decorously a little farther off. Mr. Mallory was taking the service. His deep voice rang out in the still air as he intoned the immortal phrases of the burial of the dead.

Above them all, dark against the pallor of the autumnal sky, the dragons and the devils on the church roof thrust out their grinning heads. Evan, glancing up at them, remembered that they had planned some such scene in the picture. Vashti was to be buried secretly, by moonlight, by her lover and his servant, under the eyeless gaze of the stone gargoyles. Latimer and Sturt between them could be relied on to get the last ounce of horror out of the scene.

He was standing at the back of the crowd. A slackening of tension and a general movement towards the lych-gate told him that the ceremony was over. The Condamine family had entered their car and been driven away, other cars followed and the tenants and villagers who had come on foot dispersed, some lingering to look at the wreaths and crosses, stacked up against the church wall. Evan was glad to see that there were several bunches of flowers from cottage gardens. George, he thought, would be pleased with those. Condamine had not been a model landlord, the derelict state of the village proved that, and probably he had seldom had any ready money for repairs. But he had been good-natured and easy-going. Not a man to make enemies. And yet . . .

Evan had his dinner alone that evening at the table in the window. Latimer and Sturt had been out all day and had not returned. Mrs. Price, seeing him through the serving hatch, thought he looked tired and depressed, and contrived to send him a double portion of chicken and an unusually large helping of trifle, but Evan, eating mechanically, his thoughts elsewhere, remained unaware of these marks of her favour. There were two men, newcomers to the hotel, sitting at the next table, and they were still there when most of the other diners had gone their ways.

After a while one of them spoke to Evan.

"Could I trouble you for a match? My lighter isn't working—"

"Certainly."

The stranger edged his chair a little nearer. When his cigarette was alight he said, "What do people do with themselves here in the evenings?"

He was a man of about fifty, with a slim, active-looking figure, hands tanned by the sun but noticeably well kept, a lean brown face with shrewd grey eyes and a humorous mouth. He had a quiet unhurried manner and a friendly smile. His companion was a man of heavier build, with a broad, red, good-humoured face and fists like hams.

Evan had hardly noticed them during dinner. He realized now that he had seen them before. During the inquest they had been sitting not far from him at the back of the room, and later he had seen them in the churchyard. His startled mind leapt at a conclusion.

"Excuse me—are you the police?"

"Oh dear," said the other ruefully, "does it stick out so far? But, of course you were at the inquiry, weren't you, and at the funeral. May I ask what your interest is?"

"I work for the Perivale Film Studios who are making a picture at Baring St. Mary. Mr. Condamine was helping us. I hardly knew him really. My name is Hughes, Evan Hughes. Stephen Latimer is directing and I am his assistant."

"Thank you, Mr. Hughes. I am Inspector Hugh Collier of New Scotland Yard, and this is Sergeant Duffield, who is my assistant."

"The Yard, eh? Why aren't the local people handling it?"

Collier smiled. "Sheer kindness of heart, Mr. Hughes. They wanted to give me a nice holiday in a part of the country I specially like." His smile faded. "Tell me, Mr. Hughes, were you surprised by the medical evidence this morning?"

"I was completely bowled over," said Evan, and wondered as he said it if he was being too emphatic. "It must have been some sort of accident. Not impossible in that sort of a household. The only servants a married couple, with the man working in the garden and cleaning the car. I remember noticing an opened parcel of bulbs and a very muddy pair of gardening gloves lying on a chest in the hall the first time we entered the house. It's feasible, isn't it, that weed-killer or something might get brought in."

"You think that's more likely than murder?" said Collier bluntly, and noticed that the little Welshman shied at the word like a frightened horse.

"Oh yes," he said quickly. "Yes, I do. Condamine was a most likeable fellow. It—it really is inconceivable."

"But you hardly knew him, Mr. Hughes. Appearances can be deceptive. When did you see him last, by the way?"

"Just over a fortnight ago. He took me up Dancing Hill to show me the view. We were talking most of the time about the picture. The story is founded on a tragic incident in his family history. He took us around showing us where things happened. He was very keen, and looking forward tremendously to seeing the finished film. He was as excited as a child about it. Latimer had gone back to Town and I joined him the following day. We've been hard at it ever since. Only a few of the out-door shots will actually be taken here, you know."

"I know very little about film-making," said Collier, "but I've heard of Latimer. I saw *Mariage à la Mode* and *Blackpool Blues* and enjoyed them both. Is it true that he gets his crowd scenes without employing thousands of extras?"

"Yes. He maintains you can do that sort of thing by suggestion and by using crowd noises and appropriate music. You remember the Tyburn scene in *Mariage à la Mode*, the execution of Silvertongue."

"I could have sworn there was a big crowd in that."

"No. You saw it through seven or eight spectators at a window. It was reflected to you through their eyes, their comments."

"By Gad, you're right. That's clever."

Evan flushed with pleasure. "Latimer is a genius," he said proudly.

"I'm looking forward to meeting him. I hope this trouble isn't going to affect your work. It can't be very easy to find a new subject and setting. How do you set about it?"

"There is no hard-and-fast rule. As a matter of fact Latimer has been looking out for a subject all this summer. Time was getting short and he was getting desperate when he heard the Condamine story."

"Did Mr. Condamine send up the script neatly typed, with a stamped and addressed envelope? Is that how it's done?"

"No. Mrs. Condamine sometimes stays in London with a married sister. The sister and her husband are friends of Latimer's. He met her at their flat and she happened to mention George Condamine's ambition. Latimer thought it sounded as if it might be his cup of tea. He was asked down for the week-end. Latimer liked it and so we got going."

"Running smoothly, I hope. No snags?"

Evan grinned. "Not more than one expects. Mrs. Condamine wanted a part. She might have been pretty good in it, too, though she has no experience, but it wouldn't have done. Latimer put his foot down, and she took it very well. It must be dull for a young woman like that, buried in the country."

"Is she much younger than her husband?"

"About twenty years, I should think."

"No children?"

"No."

Collier suppressed a yawn. "Time we turned in, Duffield. Good night, Mr. Hughes. I've enjoyed our chat. It's nice to get away from one's own shop some-times."

"Poor little chap," said Duffield dreamily as the mattress of his bed creaked under his weight. They were sharing a small room on the top floor as all the other rooms available had been booked for the film unit. "He's scared. He's badly scared. I wonder why."

"So do I," said Collier, "but it may be nothing to do with our job. It can't be if he was telling the truth."

"Ah, but was he?"

"Not all of it, perhaps. I don't like the look of this case. Nasty."

"That's why the locals wished it on to us. But the film stuff will make a pleasant change. We shall soon be surrounded by ravishing blondes." And cheered by this agreeable prospect the sergeant fell asleep. Collier, on the other hand, lay awake for some time. He was always keyed up at the beginning of a new case. And he had a horror of poisoning. A cold, cruel, treacherous business.

Chapter VIII
THE AWKWARD NUMBER

Ida Condamine came in from the garden with a basket full of Michaelmas daisies and was arranging them in the big jar on the refectory table in the entrance hall. The front door was open and the morning sun streamed in, revealing the beauty of the carved oak Jacobean staircase and the linenfold panelling, the shabbiness of the rugs and curtains, and the dust and disorder everywhere.

"Mrs. Condamine?"

Ida turned her head to look at the two men standing on the threshold.

"Yes. What do you want?"

The younger of the two took a step forward. "I am sorry to trouble you at such a time, but we are enquiring into the circumstances of your husband's death, and we hope you may be able to help us. You have heard, of course, of the medical evidence—"

"Yes. I had a letter from our solicitor by this morning's post, and Oswald Condamine, my husband's nephew, heard about it last night and came in and told me. I simply couldn't believe it. Are you the police or the insurance people?"

"The police, madam. I am Inspector Collier, and this is my colleague Sergeant Duffield."

"Are you from Wells or Bath?"

"From New Scotland Yard. The local people are rather short-handed just now, so the Chief Constable asked us to take over."

"I see. You had better come in here."

She led the way into a small room on the left of the front door. George had called it his study and used it when he wanted to work over his accounts, or tie flies, or merely to smoke a pipe and doze over a bulb catalogue or the local paper. It was even dustier than the hall and smelt of leather, stale tobacco smoke and dog. There were muddy footmarks, long since dry, George's footmarks, on the faded Axminster. A more sensitive and imaginative woman might have visualized George himself sitting in the armchair.

"Please sit down if you want to." She settled herself on the wide window-sill, a slim black-clad figure, her face an ivory wedge between the swinging curtains of blue-black hair.

Collier was not unusually susceptible to physical beauty, but he had to overcome a tendency to sit gaping at her. He pulled himself together in time to hear her saying, "It was a terrible shock to me. I can't understand it."

He glanced round the untidy room, at the piles of old newspapers, old letters, odd gloves, gnawed bones and bits of string, and said, "Could it have been an accident? Do you keep any arsenic, or arsenical compound in the house?"

"I suppose you mean fly-papers or weed-killer? They may have had fly-papers in the kitchen during the hot weather. We get a lot of flies then. Lucy Arden would know. And I dare say Trask uses weed-killer. He would if it saves trouble. He's awfully lazy. But I should think he would keep it outside somewhere."

"Just so. I'll talk to him presently. Meanwhile, could you tell me how Mr. Condamine spent that last day before he was taken ill?"

"It was a lovely day, and we went for a picnic. We drove along the Bristol road and turned off towards Shipham, and left the car and walked over the hills and sat down for a while and ate our sandwiches. Rather a cold wind sprang up about three o'clock, so we went back to the car. I came straight home, but I dropped George on the way at the Rectory. He wanted to have a word with Mr. Mallory about something, and I think he had a cup of tea there. I didn't see him again until just before supper. We have a sort of scratch meal about half-past seven when we're alone. He said he felt queer and thought he had caught a chill and would be better in bed. I went up myself at about ten. I had been asleep some time when I heard him calling. I put on a dressing-gown and went to him. The poor darling had been frightfully sick. I called Lucy Arden, and she got some hot water for a bottle and we cleaned up and got him into fresh pyjamas. I thought he would doze off and be all right, but it all started again. After a while we got really frightened and I made Lucy go down to the village and ring up the doctor from the post office. But he came too late."

"Terrible," said Collier sympathetically. "I notice you say you made your cousin go to ring up the doctor. Was there any conflict of opinion about the urgency of the case?"

"Not really. But I got the impression that she thought I was making a fuss. She's always rather slow off the mark, poor girl, she can't help it."

"I see. Now you'll appreciate, Mrs. Condamine, that it's very important for us to know exactly what your husband had to eat and to drink during that last day. About that picnic lunch. What did it consist of?"

"Well, there was a thermos flask of coffee which we shared between us, and we each had a packet of sandwiches. George's was corned beef and mine was a savoury filling of grated cheese and chopped chives and things. Lucy Arden is very proud of her sandwich mixtures, but I sometimes find them rather messy and I didn't touch mine. I just had a slice of cake."

"What happened to them?"

She smiled. "Oh, they weren't wasted. George ate them." Her smile vanished. "Oh, you don't think—"

"We aren't thinking," said Collier, "we're collecting facts. Miss Arden prepared the sandwiches?"

"Yes. We have a sort of cook-housekeeper person, but she had gone to her married daughter in Taunton."

"Did Mr. Condamine eat sweets?"

"No. He always gave me his sweet ration."

"Did he have a drink when he came in that afternoon?"

"I don't know. I shouldn't think so. He didn't often drink between meals. A glass of cider sometimes. There's a barrel in the cellar. But he wouldn't be thirsty just after tea at the Rectory."

"You say the cook-housekeeper was away that day. Who was in the house?"

"Just Lucy Arden. She's a distant relative of my husband. She had a job, I believe she was a dispenser, but she had a nervous breakdown. She came here before I married George and she's been here ever since."

"So the household consisted of Mr. Condamine and you and Miss Arden, and the cook-housekeeper."

"And her husband who looks after the garden."

"Thank you, Mrs. Condamine. Just one more question. Was your husband in his usual spirits on that last day?"

"Oh yes. He was very cheerful. He was so pleased about this film business. I expect you will have heard that they are making a picture founded on something that happened here three hundred years ago. My husband has spent years over it, finding out things in old letters and diaries and all that. I think at first he meant to write a book about it. I believe he did try but he hadn't got the knack of writing. He told me that as soon as he sat down with a pen and a sheet of paper his mind became a blank. He wasn't at all clever, poor sweet. He felt this picture idea was much better. He was frightfully keen."

"How did he get in touch with the film people?"

"Well, actually it was through me. I sometimes spend a few days in London with a married sister, and I met a man at her place who is a well-known director. I happened to mention George's idea to him, and he was interested."

"Just so. Thank you, Mrs. Condamine, for being so helpful. I won't take up any more of your time now. Could I see Miss Arden?"

"She's gone into Wells to do the shopping, but she will be back before lunch."

"Meanwhile, if you don't mind, we will search the house. It's just routine. We shall make as little disturbance as possible and leave everything as we found it."

She shrugged her shoulders. "By all means. What do you hope to find? Little packets of arsenic? Or would it be in a bottle? I'm afraid I'm very ignorant. Go to it. I never lock up anything. I don't know what Lucy does. I shall be in the garden if you want me."

"She's right," said Duffield when they had been through the rooms on the ground floor. "If it's an inside job the person who did it isn't going to be such a fool as to keep the stuff in his or her bedside table drawer."

"I don't know about that. Remember Armour and the packets of arsenic in his waistcoat pocket to kill the dandelions. But I don't expect to find anything here. I want to get a line on these people, and their background is going to help. The Superintendent at Wells said he thought the Condamines were hard up, but this staircase would fetch almost anything they liked to ask from a dealer in touch with the American market."

From the landing window they saw Ida Condamine lying in a hammock under an apple tree, reading a novel. "Good-looking girl," said Duffield gruffly.

Collier grinned. "A masterpiece of understatement. In the current idiom, cartloads of oomph. Condamine was a lucky man—or was he? No domestic virtues, I fear."

They had entered the large front bedroom. The bed had not been made. Clothes were scattered everywhere. Powder had been spilt over the polished mahogany of the dressing-table and there were cigarette ends stained with lipstick in the fireplace and in the saucer of the coffee cup on the breakfast tray which had been left on a chair.

"Smells nice," said Duffield.

They went rapidly and expertly through the drawers and the wardrobe and looked into the numerous handbags, but they found no powder but the powder of Coty.

George Condamine's room was at the end of the corridor, divided from that of his wife by a bathroom which had once been a powdering closet, and a spare room. It was simply furnished with a threadbare carpet and faded curtains. The only pictures were a large framed photograph of Ida Condamine on the mantelpiece and a rather blurred snapshot of a spaniel dog.

"That looks like the dog that little Welshman brought with him into the dining-room last night. Did you notice him? He was very quiet, lying under the table."

"It's the same dog. The name is written on the mount. Punch. I heard Hughes calling him. That's interesting."

In George's room they had lowered their voices instinctively. They found nothing remarkable. His wardrobe was not extensive and it was far from new, but the clothes were carefully mended and neatly folded.

"And now for the young woman who is so good at sandwich fillings," said Collier.

Lucy Arden's room was a feminine replica of George's, neat, and rather shabby and bare. The same snapshot of Punch adorned her mantelpiece, and there was another of a thickset man in plus fours, grinning amiably if rather foolishly at the camera.

"Would this be George?" Collier examined it with interest. "Looks a good-natured sort of blighter."

"I always think," said Duffield pensively, "that three are an awkward number."

Collier was looking out of the window. Someone was trudging up the avenue with a loaded shopping bag. "We've finished up here, I think. Let's go down and meet her."

"What about the stuff?"

"The Trask couple? Yes. Go up now and give their room the once over. I'll cope with Miss Arden until you have finished."

Collier went down to the hall, but Lucy did not appear, and after a few minutes he realized that she must have gone round to the back door. He pushed open the baize-covered door that shut off the servants' quarters from the front of the house and went down a stone-paved passage to the kitchen.

It was a big room, with a huge old-fashioned wasteful cooking range and copper, and a large dresser well stocked with china. A sewing-machine stood on a side table with a work basket and a pile of tattered novelettes and cheap weekly periodicals of the kind that purvey advice on their readers' love affairs, with dress-making and cookery hints.

Lucy was there. She had filled a kettle from the pump in the scullery and was setting it on the oil cooker. She looked up as Collier entered and then bent again to regulate the wick of the lamp before she spoke.

"Yes? What is it, please?"

He told her his name and his business while she stood quietly by the well-scrubbed table transferring the groceries she had brought from paper bags to glass jars. She was wearing a black-and-white striped cotton frock, a cheap little garment from a chain store, and her head was bare. She was one of those girls who are difficult to describe because of their chameleon quality, pretty one minute and plain the next. When compared with Ida Condamine she was insignificant. But Collier, observing her closely, thought that she looked intelligent.

"I'll answer questions, of course. Do you mind interviewing me here? I want to put on the potatoes for lunch as soon as the water boils."

"You have it all to do? The Trasks are not back yet?"

"Their daughter at Taunton is very ill. But I think they're keeping away because of—of what has happened. They don't want to be mixed up in it. Country people are very good at keeping out of any sort of mess. They mind their own business and don't interfere. That's why such unspeakable things go on sometimes in villages for a long time before the police hear about it."

Collier nodded. He knew that was true. He said, "We shall bring them back if they are needed. About last Monday, Miss Arden. I think we must assume that there was arsenic in something Mr. Condamine ate or drank during the day. Can you make any suggestions?"

Before she could answer Duffield came in, said "Good morning, miss", selected a chair, planked it down where the light would fall over his left shoulder, and produced his notebook.

Lucy, observing these preparations, smiled rather uncertainly. "He went out in the car with Mrs. Condamine. They took a picnic lunch with them. A thermos of coffee and sandwiches. Ida was home for tea, but she had dropped George at the Rectory and I suppose he had tea there with Mr. Mallory. He came in a little before seven and complained of feeling unwell. He went to bed."

"Did he have anything to drink then? A little whisky perhaps?"

"Not to my knowledge."

"About the sandwiches now—"

"I made corned beef sandwiches for George, but Ida doesn't care for corned beef so I put up another packet for her with a cheese and tomato filling."

"Cheese and tomato. Anything else?"

"I beat up the cheese with a little salad-dressing into a thick paste and added finely chopped chives. I used a fresh tomato and added a pinch of salt and pepper. I rather pride myself on my sandwich fillings. You—you don't think—"

"Where did you carry out this job?"

"Here. On this table."

"And where were the ingredients kept? All the stuff, the bread, butter, corned beef, everything."

"In the larder. Over there." She pointed to a door.

Collier went over and opened it. The larder was large and cool, with a stone-paved floor and slate shelves. The window opened on the yard.

"Flies could get in," remarked Collier.

"There is a wire screen we put up in the summer. There aren't many flies now, and we keep things covered."

He closed the door and came back to the table.

"Was the window open on Monday?"

"Yes. It always is. Only a few inches since a stray cat got in and spilt the milk."

"Anyone passing outside could push it up."

"Yes, I suppose so."

"You see what I'm getting at, Miss Arden? The food might have been tampered with."

She moistened her lips. "It—doesn't seem very likely."

Collier agreed with her, but he did not say so. He put the question to her that he had already asked of Mrs. Condamine.

"Do you know of any arsenic or arsenical compound that might be used in the house or garden? It might not have been in recent use. People are sometimes untidy and careless."

"Mrs. Trask had fly-papers in August when there were a lot of flies. Trask may use weed-killer. I think he did last summer, but not since. It killed some of the box edging and George was quite cross about it."

"Thank you. Shall you be staying on at Little Baring, Miss Arden?"

"No."

"Wouldn't Mrs. Condamine be glad of your company?"

"Mrs. Condamine will be leaving herself. The property is entailed. Oswald Condamine will be taking over."

"Who is that?"

"George's nephew. George's younger brother Luke married and died young. His widow and her boy lived here at the Manor until two years ago when George married. They have lived at a cottage down the road since then."

"I see. We won't take up any more of your time now. I'm afraid we shall be bothering you again later on. I should be glad if you would remain here for a few days at any rate. If you do move let the police at Wells know your address. You will be called as a witness when the inquest is resumed. We'll go out through the yard, I think. Good morning."

Collier cast an approving eye at the solidly built coach-house and farm buildings with their red-tiled roofs and doors of weathered oak. The place was beautiful even in decay, but the row of empty stalls, the grass growing between the stones, showed that life was absent.

"No riding or carriage horses, no poultry, no cows in the byre or pigs in the sty. Just a four-seater in the garage, some packets of dried eggs and rashers from the grocer's. A pity."

They entered the walled kitchen garden and looked into the potting shed where Trask kept his gardening implements. There was a tin of solignum on the shelf but no weed-killer.

"What do you think as far as we've got, Duffield?"

Duffield cleared his throat. "At present it looks as if that Miss Arden had meant to polish off the wife and slipped up owing to Mrs. C. not having fancied the cheese filling."

Collier sighed. "The obvious conclusion is often the right one. It's pretty obvious that the lovely Mrs. Condamine gave the poor relation hell. She didn't trouble to hide the contempt she felt for a young woman so hope-lessly lacking in glamour. A case of the turning worm. But she couldn't be sure that Condamine wouldn't eat some of his wife's sandwiches—as he did. Would she have taken such a risk?"

"She might have meant to kill them both," suggested Duffield.

Collier shook his head. "She was fond of George."

They were moving towards the avenue. "Look—" said Duffield. Ida Condamine was beckoning to them from her hammock.

"Well?" she said pleasantly as Collier approached, the sergeant lingering a few paces behind. "Have you finished?"

"Not exactly." Collier stood looking down at her, a little at a loss. It crossed his mind that perhaps he should warn her.

"In your place," he said, "I would be careful."

"I will," she said, and then, in a half whisper, "Thank you, Inspector."

He was silent, looking at her. She raised her eyes to his anxiously.

"It's really true? There's no mistake?"

"I'm afraid not."

"I—I'm frightened."

He hesitated. "I must ask you to stay in the neighbour-hood for a few days, but not necessarily in this house. You could go to friends, perhaps."

She shook her head. "No," she said more firmly. "You're kind. I shall feel safe, knowing you are about."

Collier was a married man who happened to be still in love with his wife, but he was only human, and it must be admitted that as he walked down the avenue he felt rather pleased with himself. Duffield, trudging stolidly by his side, broke in upon his reverie.

"Where next?" he enquired.

"The Rectory, I think."

Mr. Mallory was at home. The elderly housekeeper showed them into the shabby book-lined living-room and he came to them from the garden where he had been attending to a bonfire of weeds: tall and gaunt in his black cassock, and bringing with him the sharp acrid smell of smoke.

"The police, isn't it? I saw you in the churchyard yesterday and wondered who you were. I hadn't heard then about the result of the post-mortem. A ghastly business. Incredible."

"Everybody says that," remarked Collier. "I gather that he wasn't a man who made enemies."

"Good Heavens, no! He was a most likeable person. I shall miss him more than I can say."

"You are old friends?"

"I did not know him before I came here, but that is over twenty years ago. We became great friends, and remained so, though, of course, since his marriage I haven't seen quite so much of him."

"He married rather late in life?"

"Yes. It was rather unexpected. His sister-in-law, Mrs. Luke Condamine, kept house for him and her son lived at Little Baring with them, and there was Lucy Arden, too. I fancy they were all surprised, and not too pleased. That was only natural. He met her while he was away on a holiday and was completely bowled over. And that was natural too," said the rector with a faint smile, "as you'll agree when you see her. But, of course, you did see her yesterday. She bore up very well, I thought."

"She will be left comfortably off, I suppose."

"I hope so, but I doubt it. Like most land-owners, Condamine had very little ready money, and Little Baring is entailed. Luckily the poor dear fellow had just been paid a substantial sum by a film company. You will have heard about that perhaps?"

"Yes."

"He was very excited about it. I was rather worried. I feared it might lead to dissension between him and his wife. I gathered that she had set her heart on playing one of the principal parts. It would have been very unsuitable."

"Do you mean she would have been a flop? I should have thought that with her looks—"

"Ad astra? I think it quite possible. The road to Hollywood. And that would have been very hard on George, and not, I fear, very good for her."

"An unworldly point of view."

"What else do you expect from me?"

"Oh, of course." Collier looked at Mr. Mallory thoughtfully.

"But you wouldn't take any actual steps to prevent it?"

"Probably not. Certainly not, without prayer. One would have to be very sure."

Was there a touch of fanaticism in the rector's make-up? The lean face, heavily lined, and the blue eyes, deep-set in their bony sockets, were not altogether in keeping with the easy genial manner. Collier envisaged certain possibilities, and passed on.

"Little Baring seems to be understaffed," he said. "I could not help noticing that the place was—well—not very spick and span—did Mr. Condamine do any farming himself?"

"He grew vegetables, and there's a certain amount of fruit. But the farms were all let to tenants. Why?"

"I was thinking of a case some years ago where a man died of arsenical poisoning. After a long inquiry it was established that his death was accidental. He worked on a farm and had a good deal to do with sheep, and there is arsenic in sheep-dip. His wife was a slattern, and he was careless himself. Whether he actually brought the stuff into the house and spilt it on a shelf or on the table where they had their meals or whether he merely ate with unwashed hands remained uncertain, but there was evidence enough of negligence to satisfy the jury."

"Far fetched," thought Duffield, listening to this improvization, but it seemed to appeal to the rector.

"Ah," he said, with evident satisfaction. "I should not be surprised if you're not getting near the truth. It seems far more likely than anything else. You're right. The place is full of odds and ends. Condamine had no idea of order or method. His pockets were always stuffed with the most extraordinary collection of junk, like a small boy's. Old letters, bits of string, fossils he picked up on the hills, nuts, crumbs of bread for the birds. And he worked a lot in the garden. Weed-killer, Inspector. There you are. Your problem's solved."

"I hope you are right, Mr. Mallory. We shall see what Trask has to say about it. Thank you for being so cooperative." The rector asked them to stay to lunch but did not press the invitation. He went with them to the gate.

"I feel much happier now," he said. "I feel that this black cloud is lifting. I shall still have lost my dear old friend, but the added horror—"

"Whistling in the dark to keep his spirits up," said Duffield, when they were out of hearing.

"One of those three monkeys," said Collier. "He thinks no evil. Or shall we say that he tries not to. People you know and like, whose hands you have grasped, whose salt you have eaten. Salt, eh? A white powder—"

He stopped short. "Wait a minute." He turned back, and the rector, who had just been moving away, came back to meet him.

"Mr. Condamine came to see you on Monday afternoon. They had been for a motor run, and Mrs. Condamine dropped him here?"

"That is so."

"Did he complain of feeling unwell? I understand that he had tea with you."

"No. I was out and, as he seemed to be disappointed, my housekeeper suggested that he should wait for me. Unfortunately I was detained. I was visiting a sick woman at one of the outlying farms. He was gone when I returned, and he had left no message. He had nothing to eat or drink here. My housekeeper offered to make him a cup of tea but he declined."

"Was the question of Mrs. Condamine having a part in his film still in dispute?"

"I don't think so. I think she had quite given up the idea, the was being more sensible about it than I had anticipated."

"I should like to ask your housekeeper one or two questions."

"Certainly. Here she is."

The woman who had admitted the visitors had come out on the front doorstep. "Your dinner be on the table," she shouted.

"Come here a minute, Mrs. Samways."

She came reluctantly, wiping her hands on her apron.

"I don't want to be mixed up with nothing," she announced.

"You won't be," Collier assured her. "I just want to know if you noticed anything unusual about Mr. Condamine the last time you saw him, when he called here on Monday afternoon."

"Well, I did then. He looked rough, terrible rough—"

"She means ill," interpolated the rector.

"And he seemed upset like, and low in his mind. 'A nice cup of tea'll do 'ee good,' I said, but he said, 'No tea. I feel sick,' he said. 'It's the shock,' he said, more to himself as it were, 'mind over matter,' he said. I left him in the sitting-room and now and again I heard him groaning and saying, 'My God!' and then presently he called to me that he couldn't stop no longer. I was busy ironing and I didn't go to let him out seeing as he knew his way."

The rector looked distressed. "Why didn't you tell me all this when I came in, Mrs. Samways? I would have gone over that same evening."

"You'd had a long day, sir. You was fair wore out."

"You did wrong. You must never keep me in the dark."

Mrs. Samways' wrinkled face twitched. "I'm sorry for it now, sir. But how was I to know the Squire was a murdered man?"

The rector put up his hands as if thrusting something away from him. "No! No! No!" he cried. "Not that." Collier left them and walked back very slowly and thoughtfully to rejoin the sergeant, who had been waiting patiently by the lych-gate.

CHAPTER IX
THE LAST DAY

"IF YOU are journalists," said Mrs. Luke through the slit of the letter-box, "I know nothing and have nothing to say."

"We are the police, madam. If you will open the door I will show you my warrant card."

Julia Condamine was fond of saying that she had expressed her personality in the interior decoration of the cottage which had been lent to her indefinitely by her brother-in-law when she and her son left the Manor after his marriage. The door was painted peacock blue to match the cushions on the divan. The window curtains were orange and white and there was an orange-and-white hearthrug. The only picture on the cream distempered walls was van Gogh's "Sunflowers". Arty, thought Collier, with the art of the day before yesterday. She keeps the place clean, though.

"I hope you didn't think it very odd my keeping you out like that," she said with a nervous little laugh. "Do sit down. A man came a little while ago from some newspaper, and I had a difficulty in getting rid of him. Like these people who want to buy gold—as if one had any. It's about poor George, of course. So awful. Have you made an arrest?"

Her eyes and teeth glittered as she leaned eagerly towards them.

"Not yet," said Collier. "We are collecting information. Can you help us at all, Mrs. Condamine?"

"One hardly likes to accuse anyone—" she began.

Collier interrupted her. "We don't want accusations. Perhaps if I put a few questions. You saw a good deal of the deceased, no doubt."

"Oh yes. He often dropped in here, and my son and I were in and out of the Manor most days. It is nearly a mile by road, but much nearer across the park, and there is a door in the wall at the end of our little back garden. This used to be two cottages, and a gamekeeper, and one of the gardeners lived here. Years ago when wages weren't so impossible. Dear George. He always said there was such an atmosphere of peace here. He was very loyal. He never said much, but of course I knew that things were often difficult for him."

"How was that?"

"Oh dear! I don't want to make mischief. It was simply that he had married a woman more than twenty years younger than he was and with quite different tastes. The country bores her. She wants crowds, excitement, change, admiration. She feels she is buried alive here. It's natural. But what I say is she shouldn't have married him if that was what she wanted. It was too bad to make him unhappy by sulking and whining and finding fault. He gave her all he could. He's not a rich man."

"I suppose when she married she was in love, and didn't realize the drawbacks," suggested Collier.

"She realized the advantages," said Mrs. Luke.

"She would have settled down when the children came along," said Collier, with a man's greater tolerance for a pretty woman's vagaries.

Mrs. Luke frowned and her restless fingers jerked irritably at her long dangling chain of jet and crystal beads.

"I doubt if children were ever a part of her plan. But we need not consider that now."

"No. No, I suppose not. Well, she need not go on living here if she does not like it. She could let the place or sell it."

"No. George will have made some provision for her, but Little Baring is entailed. It comes to my son."

"I see." Collier paused. "You will understand, Mrs. Condamine, that in a case like this we must look for a motive, we must ask ourselves—and try to find out from other people—who had anything to gain from the death of the victim."

Mrs. Luke's sallow face flushed. "I hope you are not suggesting that Oswald murdered his uncle to get Little

Baring. I can tell you that he is dismayed at the prospect of being a landowner. He is young, gay, irresponsible, he has the temperament of an artist. Material possessions mean nothing to him. If you can't do better than that I'm afraid you won't get very far."

"Please don't misunderstand me," said Collier soothingly. "I did not mean anything personal." He realized that he would not get anything more from her then, and rose. "Could I have a word with your son before I go?"

"He is out. He went off on his motor-cycle directly after breakfast. He often runs over to Weston to bathe and go to a cinema. There isn't much for him to do here."

Collier reflected that he might have done something to the neglected garden. A spoiled cub. He said, "Will you ask him to run over to Wells and call at the police station some time this evening? I shall be there, or not far off. I should like to talk over some aspects of the case with him. I am assuming that he is as anxious to clear up the mystery of his uncle's death as we are." He had dropped his friendly for his official manner, and observed with interest that she looked frightened.

"Very well," she said.

"By the way, when did you last see Mr. Condamine alive?"

"Sunday afternoon. He had taken Punch for a run and he came in for a few minutes on his way home."

"Was he in good spirits?"

"Oh, very. He was looking forward to the arrival of the film unit and to seeing some of the shots taken. He came to me for sympathy. Ida was inclined to snub him when he talked about it. I fancy she had expected to be offered a part, but it did not materialize. I suppose the director did not think her good enough. These film-struck young women," said Mrs. Luke, with her patronizing little laugh.

"I don't know what you think," said Collier as he and the sergeant walked along the road towards the corner where they hoped to catch a bus back to Wells, "but if I was Mrs. George Condamine I should feel very inclined to murder my sister-in-law."

"Spiteful, wasn't she," Duffield agreed.

"I've got that larder window on my mind. You'd better go back after we've had a spot of lunch, and go over it thoroughly inside and out for finger-prints. See if it's overlooked and if any moderately active person could climb in and out again. Then get the dabs of everyone we've interviewed this morning."

"Make some excuse or ask them outright?"

"Ask them. They may as well know they're all suspects. It's a good plan sometimes to put the wind up people. They get flustered and make mistakes."

"We haven't seen everybody yet."

"No. I asked the local people to find out what they could about the Trask couple. I may run over to Taunton to give them the once over while you're collecting prints. And this evening, I hope, we'll put the young gentleman with the artistic temperament through the mangle. And here, thank heaven, is the bus. I'm hungry."

After a hurried meal at the hotel they parted company and Collier called at the police station where a car with a driver was ready to take him to Taunton. The Trasks had been located. They were staying in lodgings not far from the hospital where their daughter, who had undergone an operation, was still on the danger list. The police report on them was favourable. They had both been in service with the Condamines since they left school at the age of fourteen and had remained on after their marriage, although for the first few years they had lived at the lodge and Mrs. Trask had only gone up to the house to give extra help when needed. Trask was honest and a good worker, but slow and not particularly bright. His wife had the brains. A fine upstanding female, the local inspector allowed.

When Collier saw her he agreed. She came to the door of the little house, one of a terrace. She had the mellow ample beauty that is characteristic of many of the country-women of Somerset, a beauty of warm colouring and noble lines and a placid dignity. Not Junoesque, a kinder goddess, Ceres perhaps. He saw that she had been crying.

He told her who he was and she showed him into the small and over-furnished front parlour.

"Sit down, sir. Us be in trouble, as maybe you'll have heard, about our Millie. My husband's gone to the hospital now, but he'll be back soon. Her's only allowed one visitor at a time, and I was with her this morning. And now this bad news about Squire. For the dear Lord's sake, sir, tesn't true that he died of poison?"

"I'm afraid it is."

"This is what comes of raking up they mucky old stories that are best put out of mind. I told the master no good 'ud come of such doings, but he only laughed."

"Are you referring to the film project?"

She looked at him steadily. "You don't believe me. 'Tis true though. There was ill-wishing in those bygone times, and laying on of charms, and a calling of names that should never be spoken. All dead, and buried and forgotten, and a good thing, too. But he wouldn't rest until he'd dug 'em up and brought 'em back to life."

Collier did not argue the point. He said bluntly, "There was arsenic in something he ate or drank on Monday. Arsenic might be derived from fly-papers or weed-killer. Can you help me about that?"

"We used fly-papers in the kitchen in August, but not since then. They was kept in a dresser drawer, but there weren't none left. I mind hanging up the last. And the last time we had weed-killer was two years back. Mr. George said us weren't to put down no more after he found a dead thrush on the path. Very tender-hearted Mr. George is. Was, I should say." Her lips quivered. "I can't believe he's gone. How'm they doing up at the Manor, sir? I wish I was there to help Miss Lucy, but I can't leave my daughter."

He noticed that she showed no concern for Mrs. Condamine, but that might be explained as the natural antagonism of old servants to a new mistress. He asked her a few more questions, but her answers threw no fresh light on his problem.

He went back to his waiting car and told the driver to stop at the first public telephone-box.

He rang up the office of Rand, Quinton and Rand, and after a brief delay, heard the precise voice of the elderly solicitor who had given evidence at the inquest on George Condamine.

"Who did you say? An Inspector from Scotland Yard? Particulars of Mr. Condamine's will? I can hardly give them over the phone. You had better come to see me. Yes, this evening if it is urgent. I live over the office. Any time after eight will suit me. Good-bye."

Collier went back to Wells and spent the hour before dinner in his room writing up his report. Duffield had been awaiting his return. He had obtained five sets of finger-prints. No one had seemed to mind giving them, and the rector had expressed keen interest in the process.

"Young Condamine was at home then. What did you think of him?"

"Fat flabby type," said Duffield distastefully. "Called me dear. Me!"

"Mother's darling."

"Oh, no doubt about that. Dearest Ozzie."

"What about the larder window and shelves? Did you get any prints there?"

"Sorry. None. The surfaces were very rough on the window frame and sill, and Miss Arden told me the shelves are wiped down with a damp cloth every day."

They were the first to go down to the dining-room and were having their soup when Evan Hughes came in with two other men. The waiter, bringing their fish, said in awed tones, "That's the film director, that's Mr. Latimer in the green shirt."

Latimer was leaning back in his chair smoking a cigarette. He seemed sulky and irritable, and it was obvious that his companions were handling him carefully. Collier, who remembered him in the part of lawyer Silvertongue in *Mariage à la Mode*, would not have known him, but in the film he had worn a wig or powder, and his untidy mane of chestnut-coloured hair added greatly to the general impression of a rather dangerous and feral charm. A man, thought Collier, who could be generous or cruel, who would be loved—and feared. Seeing him, he began to understand the evident dog-like devotion of the little Welshman. Without appearing to listen, he managed to overhear a word here and there.

"The kid's shaping well, Latimer; she'll take well. Don't drive her too hard. She was nearly crying more than once this afternoon."

"That's what I want. Real tears. She'll go through those brambles to-morrow. What are a few scratches? I'm only showing a few glimpses of the howling mob that's hunting her down. It's up to her to put the mob over with the audience. Her acting and Heppenstall's music. He knows what I want and he's writing it now."

Collier looked at his watch. Time to be moving. He did not want to annoy Mr. Rand by arriving late. He got up and left the dining-room, followed by Duffield.

When they were gone, Latimer drew a long breath. "Were those the cops, Bunny?"

"Yes."

"The large beefy-faced one is typical, the other less so. Well, their activities shouldn't affect us."

The September evening had turned chilly, and Mr. Rand, having dined, was sitting by a small wood fire sipping his coffee when his elderly manservant announced the two visitors.

He shook hands with them and asked them to be seated. "And now what is it that you want to know?"

"Briefly, sir, the terms of Mr. Condamine's will."

"Certainly. Failing a direct heir, a son of his own, the estate of Great and Little Baring, including the Manor house and its contents, go to his nephew, Oswald Condamine. Mrs. Ida Condamine, the widow, gets a life interest of three hundred a year chargeable to the estate. There are legacies of fifty pounds each to Trask and his wife. That is all."

"Nothing to his sister-in-law?"

"No. He said to me that her boy would look after her, and no doubt he will."

"I think you said he made this will quite recently. Is it very different to the previous one?"

"He left more to Lucy Arden. Oh, I beg your pardon—I had not mentioned her as one of the legatees. I can't think how I came to leave her out. He has left her five hundred pounds instead of two."

"I suppose that he was, for his position, a poor man, and that when death duties have been paid and the charges on the estate met young Condamine won't have much left to play with?"

Mr. Rand was silent for a moment. Then he said, "I think he will break the entail. It can be done, you know."

"I see."

"Have you made any progress, Inspector?"

"Very little," confessed Collier.

The moon was rising as they turned west again and climbed the first long hill and left the city of Bath behind them in the winding valley of the Avon. They spoke little on the way, and when they reached the hotel they went straight up to their room. Collier was busy with his thoughts, and Duffield knew when to be silent. Collier filled his pipe while the sergeant, sighing deeply, sat down on the end of his bed and took off his shoes.

"Somebody killed him," said Collier at last. "But why? The two women who are the obvious suspects both lose by his death. Miss Arden gets a legacy, but she had a home at the Manor, and either she was genuinely fond of her cousin or she's a remarkably good actress. Of course she may be just that. Lots of women are. The money motive doesn't stand up. There may be something else. But all the evidence is that he was a kind husband and a loyal friend. Everyone liked him."

"Maybe Mrs. Condamine was right, and the poison was meant for her," suggested Duffield. "Suppose Miss Arden had been hoping to marry her cousin when the other woman came along and beat her to it. She might have tried to get rid of her now, hoping to step into her shoes."

"I've thought of that," said Collier. "It might be. We've still a long way to go."

Chapter X
WITCH HUNT

"That's the lot," said Evan, shaking the last crumb out of the paper bag. The ducks, observing him with intelligent beady eyes, accepted this, and swam away. A swan remained and Evan gazed at it dreamily and at its reflection in the dark green water. A warmer white than snow. More like whipped cream. He thought he would like to be a painter: a peaceful occupation in which one need not be inextricably involved with other human beings. "Oh, Mr. Hughes—"

Someone had come up behind him. He turned, with a sigh, for he had been cherishing his solitude, and saw Lucy Arden.

"I've just come in by the first bus, and I saw you crossing the square. It's nice here, isn't it, under the trees. Quiet."

"Yes."

"I—I don't want to bother you," she said humbly, "but I wanted to know about Punch. He—he isn't with you this morning. You haven't—" He saw the fear in her eyes and was suddenly so sorry for her that he forgot his own worries. "He's all right," he said. "Mrs. Price at the hotel was very decent about it, but I couldn't keep him with me just now. I have to be running about with, or for, Latimer. I'm boarding him out with a vet on the Glastonbury road. I'll be responsible for him until you're ready to have him. I promise you."

"Thank you."

"How are you getting on?"

"The police are always in and out. I don't mind them. They ask questions, but not in a bullying way. They—they are company," she said simply. "I'm alone so much now. Ida goes out in her car and stays out all day. She prepares her own meals and takes them up to her room on a tray. I think—I really do think she's afraid of me. I was very dense. I used to offer to make toast or scrambled eggs or something. She hates cooking. But now I realize she must really believe that I'm a—a murderess."

"Rubbish!" said Evan. "She's just putting on an act."

"Well, I've wondered that, too. Because, after all, she— but I can't bear to think it."

"You ought to get right away."

"I should like to, but it seems best to stay for the present. I've got to face facts, Mr. Hughes. I shouldn't be welcome anywhere while I'm under suspicion."

"I don't see why you should be suspected."

"It's quite natural. George and Ida went for a run that last day and took a picnic lunch with them. I prepared the sandwiches, corned beef for George, and a cheese filling for Ida. She didn't eat hers, it seems. She told the Inspector she was tired of my cheese mixture. I don't know why she didn't tell me. Anyhow, George ate them all. They seem pretty certain that the poison was in the sandwiches. I can only say that I didn't put any in."

"Of course not," said Evan warmly, but secretly he was appalled. It seemed to him as they paced slowly on under the trees, with the dead leaves rustling underfoot, that a darker shadow lay over them than was cast by the elms.

"The police took away the picnic basket that was always kept in the car. Ida wanted it and we looked everywhere before we realized what had happened. Ida—I never liked her, she's never been kind to me, she hates me, I think— but I can't help being sorry for her. I didn't think she really cared for George, but I was wrong. She's breaking her heart for him. I hear her in the night sobbing and crying."

Evan said nothing. She cannot have read his thoughts, for she went on more cheerfully, "I feel braver now. I'm glad I ran after you. You—somehow one can say things to you and feel safe. I hope you don't mind. How is the picture getting on?"

"All right so far, but it's a hectic business. We were rehearsing Vashti, the girl who's being hunted as a witch, yesterday. We'll be taking shots of her pushing her way through the undergrowth and then she comes out into a little clearing in the woods, on the side of the hill just above the pond. She has to run down there. Twice she stumbles and falls and picks herself up again, and then, when she has disappeared, the first of the crowd burst out of the wood like the leading hounds in the pack. Poor Rosamund. She was all in last night. She's spending to-day in bed. We're doing the crowd scenes to-day and to-morrow."

"Where does the crowd come from?"

Evan grinned. "It arrived an hour ago in two motor-coaches. Mrs. Price agreed to give them breakfast. They are staying the night at an hotel in Weston that specializes in bean feasts and outings, and getting the rest of their grub there. This mustn't go any farther, Lucy. It's a trade secret."

"I'll keep it."

"Latimer is a master of illusion. He can make sixty extras seem like at least fifteen hundred. Take the mob in the execution scene in *Mariage à la Mode*. We took shots of spectators at a window, of ragged urchins wriggling their way between the legs of the people, of women caught in the press as it swayed to and fro and screaming with fright, of men and boys clambering up a wall and sitting on the top. And then, of course, sound helps, the roar of a real crowd, the right kind of music."

"Won't it take a long time to make them all do the right things?"

"They've been rehearsing for a fortnight on the set at the Studios. They have to go through it this afternoon on the spot so that the camera-man can see if it's all right. Pegasus came down yesterday by road with his groom."

"Who's Pegasus?"

"The horse Latimer will ride. He belongs to the Studios and has appeared in several films. We have to have a specially trained animal who won't mind noise and people milling all round him."

"Is Mr. Latimer taking a part as well as directing?"

"Yes. He's playing Hugh Condamine. But he'll only act in one short scene on location. Most of the picture will be done on the set that is being built at the Studios."

"Oh," she said. "George would have been disappointed. He thought the shell of the old house at Great Baring would be such a fine background."

"We shall be using some distant shots of it, but when you get near it is too apparent that it is only a shell. But Latimer thinks of using it for a final shot. The ruined house and the gardens a wilderness, and on the grass-grown terrace the wraith of Vashti, laughing, her long black hair blowing in the wind.

Lucy shuddered. "Yes," she said rather faintly, "that would be effective, I suppose."

"Why don't you come and watch us at work? Keep well behind the cameras, and be as quiet as you can. No members of the public admitted, but if they try to stop you, show them this." He took a card from his notecase and scribbled on it Admit Bearer. "I must go and round up my flock."

He hurried away, leaving her to sit on a bench under the trees.

He found Latimer alone in the coffee-room eating a late breakfast and scowling over his morning mail. He thrust one letter into a pocket of his sports jacket and pushed the others over to Evan.

"Here. You're supposed to be my secretary. Cope with the film-struck junior misses who want autographs or auditions. Tell the widow with nine starving children to go to blazes. As to the bill, I believe I've still got a balance at the bank."

"All right," said Evan. "I'll attend to it to-night. The extras are here."

Latimer brightened. "Oh, good. Take them along to the clearing. I'll follow with Sturt."

Half an hour later the two motor-coaches had drawn up at a field gate in a muddy lane, and sixty people, male and female, between the ages of fourteen and seventy, were following Evan round the pond, a dim and glaucous stretch of water, reed fringed, and reflecting a grey sky, picking their way over the rough ground, and talking at the tops of their voices.

"So that's where she's going to be ducked. Poor Miss Harper. It looks cold and muddy. Glad I'm not in her shoes."

"Says you. She's got a good chance to steal the picture from our Stella. Coo. What's a drop of dirty water? Come to that, we shall get our feet wet standing about among those rushes."

"I hate working on location."

"So do I. Woods and mountains. You can have them. What is there here they couldn't build on the set in a couple of days?"

"Plenty. You can fake houses, but not woods."

Three film cameras were already in position at the side of the clearing, with a row of deck chairs for the director and his staff. Eventually the rehearsal got under way. The scenes in the clearing were enacted and re-enacted, with Evan shouting directions through a megaphone, and Latimer springing up from his chair to show his puppets exactly what he wanted from them. After no one knew how long, everyone trailed down the hill to the pond, and the shouting and the drilling was resumed. "Again. Do it again. Close up there. Press together. Push. You're straining to see something. You're fighting to catch the last bus. Put some pep into it."

All this, thought Evan, mopping his brow, for a scene that won't last more than ten minutes on the screen. Ten minutes at the outside.

The light was beginning to fail when Sturt said, "O.K., Boss. That should be good enough. If the weather holds we can shoot to-morrow. What about your scene with Miss Harper, when you ride into the pool and carry her off?"

"We'll run through it just before you take it."

The signal was given, and the extras, white with fatigue under their make-up, and sweating profusely, trudged off to the waiting coaches that were to take them to Weston for a high tea and a night's rest. Latimer stayed behind to discuss some technical details with Sturt and the other camera-men. Evan waited for him and they walked down to Latimer's car together.

"Another couple of days and we should have finished here, and be on our way back to London. Thank God for that," said Latimer in such heart-felt tones that Evan looked at him quickly.

"You were at the top of your form to-day. Those scenes as you've built them up ought to be terrific."

Latimer laid a hand on his shoulder. "You're a good chap, Bunny. I don't know what I should do without you. I've been swearing at you for hours, blaming you for everything that went wrong."

The little Welshman flushed with pleasure. "I know you don't mean it. You're just letting off steam."

"That's it. You're my safety valve. If only people would leave me alone. I'm always trying to drum it into their silly heads that my art, which happens to be making films, is the only thing I really care about. It's no use. God!" His voice rose. "I won't be involved. I won't be tied down."

He slid into the driver's seat and pressed the self-starter as Evan scrambled in after him, "I'm not going back to the hotel yet. I can't stick sitting at the next table to those two flatties. We'll run over to Bath, get some grub, and go to a movie there."

"What about those letters you wanted me to answer?"

"They'll keep."

Evan suppressed a sigh. He was aching with fatigue and his throat was sore after his exertions. He had been looking forward to going to bed early, but he knew that Latimer, after a prolonged creative effort, was quite unable to rest. He was driving much too fast, but it would not do to say so. He held on to his seat as they cut a corner.

Throughout the day, when he had had time to think at all, he had thought of Lucy. He did not think her pretty or attractive, but she was companionable. He was invariably ignored by young women with any pretensions to glamour. It was pleasant to be noticed and even, as it were, leant on, for a change. She was grateful to him for taking charge of the spaniel, she told him her troubles and said he had cheered her up. He liked her. But when she was not with him he was assailed by nagging doubts. Suppose, after all, she had rubbed a little white powder, innocent-looking stuff that might be salt or sugar, into the butter or the grated cheese before she cut those sandwiches? He knew no more of her than she had told him. He would have liked to talk over the case with Latimer, but Latimer had banned any discussion of it from the first.

"I will not be distracted from my job," he had said when Sturt made some reference to it.

It was past midnight when Evan crept at last into his bed. They had carried out the programme outlined by Latimer, dining at an hotel and going on to a cinema. Evan had dozed uneasily through the star and supporting features and had no recollection of the drive back through a silent countryside under a waning moon.

The next morning they were to start shooting. They picked up Rosamund Harper at her hotel. She was wearing a long coat over her gipsy rags and was made up for her part. Her maid was with her, carrying all that she might need for running repairs in a suitcase. Latimer, who was driving, asked her to sit beside him and turned his charm full on to conquer her evident nervousness.

"You're not dressed for your part, Stephen?"

"No. We're taking all that has to be taken in the clearing first. The scenes at the pond will come after the lunch interval. Perkins came down yesterday with my clubber in a motor trailer which is parked in a corner of the field, and I shall change there. You're not afraid? You'll be taken wading into the water up to your knees, up to your waist. Then Cut! The figure floating face downwards will be the dummy. I shall ride in and lift the dummy on to the saddle. Cut again while you take the dummy's place as I ride out of the water and the crowd divides to let me pass. Remember you are dead. Let your arms trail, let your head slip sideways. You know. We've been through all that."

"I know," she said earnestly. "I won't let you down."

"Good girl."

He glanced round, smiling, at the piquant little face. She wasn't in the same street as Ida Condamine for looks, but she was well enough, and she did what she was told without making a fuss. A good trooper.

They began with Vashti's flight, struggling through briars, stumbling, falling, picking herself up again. When, at last, Latimer said, "That will do, my dear. Cut!" blood was running down her bare arms and legs from numerous deep scratches, her eyes were staring and her mouth was open with the agony of a spent runner breasting the tape. Her dresser, who had been standing by in a state of growing indignation, muttered "Brutes!" and ran to her.

"That's right," said Latimer. "Take her to my trailer. There's a bed in it. Look after her and make her lie down. She won't be needed again until about three o'clock. Extras now."

Mrs. Luke Condamine arrived after the lunch interval, with Lucy Arden. Evan, who went to meet them as they emerged from the wood, had chairs set for them behind the row that had been placed for Latimer and his various assistants and advisers.

"You won't mind if he doesn't notice you, and please don't try to attract his attention," he said anxiously. "When we say that members of the public are not admitted we really mean it."

"The sensitive artistic type," cried Julia Condamine ecstatically. "Don't I know it. The least thing puts them off. I'm rather like that myself actually, being an artist too in my humble way, though I gave it up when I married. Isn't this exciting, Lucy? All these people dressed up. I feel myself transported to the seventeenth century, by my halidom, and all that. No, that's more Tudor."

"Try gadzooks," said Evan, grinning. The irrepressible Mrs. Luke amused him, though he sincerely hoped that she would take his hint and not attempt to engage Latimer in conversation.

The light was just what they had hoped for, sunless, with a grey sky. The air was heavy and sultry, presaging a storm later on, and most of the technicians were in their shirt sleeves. Latimer had just taken off his coat and slung it over the back of his chair before going forward to alter the grouping of a section of the crowd that was to surge across the marshy ground to the water's edge.

"I wouldn't have missed it for worlds," said Julia, "and when Lucy here seemed inclined to hang back I said, after all, I said, all this ground they are on belongs to my son now, and I fancy he might order them off it if he liked. Their agreement was with George. So I rather fancy I have a little right to be here if I choose."

Evan was so startled by this unexpected baring of teeth that he gaped at her, and then, realizing that she probably prided herself on a line of persiflage, he smiled rather feebly. "I hope you won't do anything so drastic. And seriously, Mrs. Condamine, we're delighted to have you looking on. We're only asking you to obey the rules as we should ask the Queen herself if she honoured us with a visit while a picture was being taken."

To his relief this tactful speech went down very well. Latimer called him just then as the cameras were being moved forward, and for the next hour he was far too busy even to glance towards the rising ground where he had left the two not very welcome visitors sitting behind the deserted row of deck-chairs. It was past four when the last of the crowd scenes had been shot. Rosamund Harper had emerged from the trailer and Latimer had gone in to dress. At the far end of the field Pegasus was being walked up and down by his groom. The mobile canteen attached to the unit had arrived and was besieged by hot and thirsty extras demanding cups of tea and buns. Evan, looking at his watch, reckoned he might count on ten minutes to himself before the two stars went into action, and thought it might be a good idea to take cups of tea to Mrs. Luke and Lucy, but when he looked in their direction he was not altogether sorry to see that they had gone.

He got a cup of tea for himself and was still drinking it when Latimer left the trailer wearing the brown velvet coat and full breeches and high leather boots of his costume. One of the extras, a young boy, came up to him with a note. Latimer took it with an irritable gesture, read it, and tore it up, dropping the pieces in the long grass, before he went over to speak to Rosamund Harper who was fondling Pegasus and giving him lumps of sugar. Evan joined them. "All ready?"

Rosamund looked at him. He saw that she was trembling. She said in a high brittle voice, "I'm terrified. Simply terrified."

Latimer said, "I'm not sure that we ought not to have made her drunk. Can't be helped now. Lode, darling, when I give the signal you run down through the reeds there and into the water. Run as you would if there were a bull charging after you. Damn it, I wish I'd hired a bull. There must be some about. Remember they're after you, and if they catch you you'll be torn to pieces. Drowning's easier. Stop when Evan shouts 'Cut!'"

CHAPTER XI
LOVE GROWN COLD

EVAN slept later than usual. He had been dead tired the night before. He had waited up for Latimer, who, when the shooting was over for the day, after a retake of the poignant scene in which he rode into and out of the pond carrying the body of the gipsy girl, had asked his assistant director to take Rosamund back to her hotel in one of the other cars. "Leave mine," he said before he disappeared into the trailer to get out of his wet and mud-stained clothes. "I'm going for a run. No, I don't want you, Bunny. I want to be alone."

He had been like that before after a period of gruelling hard work, but this time he had come in, after midnight, so drunk that he could hardly stand, and that was unprecedented. Evan helped him up to his room, undressed him, tucked him up in bed, and left him to sleep it off.

They were to see a run through of the scenes that had been shot during the morning, and if they were satisfactory they could leave for Town that very afternoon. And a good thing, too, thought Evan, and was dozing off again when he was roused by the chambermaid knocking at his door. "A lady to see you, sir."

"A lady? Who is it?"

"Miss Arden."

"Ask her to wait. I'll be down in ten minutes."

He found Lucy standing in the vestibule.

"They should have taken you into the lounge."

"I said I'd rather stay here. I'm afraid you'll think me a nuisance," she said tremulously.

He looked at her. "Have you had any breakfast?"

"No. I—I wanted to catch the bus—"

"Well, I haven't either. Come in here and have some with me."

It was nearly ten and the other guests had had breakfast and gone their ways. The waiter brought tea and toast and a plate of bacon and eggs, and left them.

"I hope you didn't mind Cousin Julia coming with me yesterday," she said apologetically. "She had come up to the house and was going round the rooms talking about the changes she meant to make, and at last I said I was going to watch the making of the picture—because she stayed on and on, and I didn't want to miss it—and she said she'd come with me."

"That was all right," said Evan, "it didn't matter at all. And you didn't stay very long, did you? You were gone by four."

He refilled her cup and his own and observed with satisfaction that there was a little more colour in her cheeks and lips.

"Now," he said, "what did you want to see me about?"

"I'm worried about Ida. I didn't hear her come in last night. This morning I went to her room and she wasn't there, and her bed hadn't been slept in."

"Oh—" Involuntarily Evan glanced towards the table where the Inspector from Scotland Yard and his colleague usually sat. He had wondered if they had made any progress. He hesitated.

"You think she has been arrested?"

"I don't know. She had not been at home all day, unless she came in while I was watching you at work."

"She was out in her car?"

"Yes."

"Could she have gone off on a visit to friends?"

"I thought of that. I looked in the cupboard where we kept the luggage. The suitcases are all there. I don't understand it at all."

"If—" he began, "she may have lost her nerve and just bolted. I think perhaps you should tell the police."

"She won't like that. She'll be angry."

"You're afraid of her, aren't you?"

"I am rather. But I expect you are right. I'll go round to the station now." She got up. "Thanks for the breakfast."

"Shall I come with you?"

"No. No need for you to get mixed up in it."

He went with her as far as the hotel entrance and stood watching her rather uncertainly as she crossed the street and until she turned the corner. It was time he went up to Latimer, who would be suffering from a hangover and would need careful handling if he was to be brought to the cinema for the run through.

He had ordered another pot of tea and a rack of dry toast. He took the tray from the waiter and carried it up to Latimer's room. Latimer was still in bed. He groaned and drew the clothes up over his head as Evan pulled up the blind.

"Must you do that?"

"The run through is at eleven. How do you feel?"

"Rotten." He sat up cautiously and took the tray on his knees.

"Was I very tight last night?"

"Tight as an owl."

Latimer groaned again. "I've been dreaming. Horrible dreams. Arms that turned to tentacles, that withered and grew cold and became chains. No. No toast." He drank the tea thirstily and refilled his cup unsteadily so that some was spilt on the tray. "You'll have to go to the run through, Bunny. I can't face it. My head. If you have any doubts hold everything until to-morrow. What time is it?"

"Ten to eleven."

"All right. Get going. Come back here and tell me."

"Very well." Evan hesitated. Should he mention Ida Condamine's disappearance? No. Better wait until after the run through.

When he walked back to the hotel an hour later he was in much better spirits. Stephen had done it again. He had put over what he wanted to convey. The terror, the urgency came through in those shots, and there was beauty, too. The plunging horse with its double load silhouetted against the sky. If that level could be kept up through the rest of the picture its success was assured. He found Latimer partly dressed. He had had a bath and shaved and looked better, though his eyes were bloodshot and his hand shook. He was sitting by the open window smoking and looking across the old tiled roofs and chimney stacks at the great west front of the cathedral.

"Well?"

"It's the best thing you've done, look you," cried the little Welshman eagerly. "It flows like a stream in spate and carries you with it. Sturt's delighted. You know he never says much, but he turned to me and said, 'Tell the Boss I'm proud to be working with him'."

Latimer smiled. "Good. Then we can—" he broke off as someone knocked at the door. "Come in."

"Thank you. I just wanted a few words with you. Oh, good morning, Mr. Hughes. You weren't down when the sergeant and I went out."

Evan moistened his lips. "Stephen, this is Detective-Inspector Collier."

"We're fellow guests in this pub, aren't we?" said Latimer. "Bunny, sit on the bed and give the Inspector your chair."

"Sergeant Duffield and I have been thrilled by the few incidental glimpses we have had behind the scenes," said Collier. "Our job, unfortunately, is a much less pleasant one. You are a friend of the Condamines, I believe."

"I have known Mrs. Condamine slightly for some months. I met her at her sister's flat in Kensington where I sometimes go to play bridge. I had not met any other member of the family until three weeks ago when Mr. Hughes and I spent a couple of days at the Manor to discuss the possibilities of making a film."

"You took Mrs. Condamine out now and then to dine at a restaurant?"

"Yes. What of it?"

There was a brass knob on the bedpost. Evan was twisting it round in its socket. He could see his own anxious face reflected and distorted on its convex surface. A sick monkey. Yes, definitely a sick monkey. Not a type pretty women wanted to dine with. Just as well perhaps.

"Did you take her out last night?"

"No. It can hardly have escaped your notice that I've been very busy. I've had no leisure for social amenities. I have not seen Mrs. Condamine at all this time. In any case this would hardly be the moment for comparative strangers to butt in."

Don't, thought Evan. Don't lose your temper. Don't talk too much. Just yes and no.

"Your film unit was in action all day yesterday until five o'clock. No members of the public were admitted, but several boys from the village were there peeping through gaps in the hedge; a policeman rode by twice making his rounds. I daresay there were others. At five the actors who had been running about and crowding round the pond got into two motor-coaches and were driven away. The cameras and the rest of the gear was dismantled and packed into lorries. Mr. Hughes drove back to Wells with the young lady who had been playing a leading part. You got into your car after changing into your own clothes, and drove away alone. Is that correct?"

"Quite right. But what's the big idea?"

"I'm asking the questions, Mr. Latimer. You can refuse to answer, but I don't advise it. A police investigation is a more complicated affair than it seems on the surface. My colleague and I are here, but all sorts of enquiries are being carried on elsewhere. Charwomen, porters of blocks of flats, commissionaires at night clubs. We know that you were on much more intimate terms with Mrs. Condamine than you have cared to admit. That being so, we wondered if she had taken you into her confidence before she left home."

"Left home? I don't know what you're talking about. I tell you I haven't seen her since we left the Manor nearly three weeks ago."

Collier looked at Evan. "You haven't told him?"

"No. He had a bad headache when he woke. He was due at the cinema to see a run through of the shots we took yesterday. He asked me to go instead of him. I was just going to tell him when you arrived."

"For God's sake," said Latimer in a high voice, "what's happened now?"

"Mrs. Condamine has disappeared. She went out in her car yesterday morning, and has not returned. Miss Arden came into Wells and asked Mr. Hughes' advice, and he very sensibly urged her to tell the police."

Latimer had been pale before; he had now lost the last vestige of colour. "The little fool," he muttered. "She hasn't—"

Evan spoke in a hurry. "Stephen—"

Collier glared at him. "If you can't keep quiet you'll have to leave the room. You won't help your friend by trying to prevent him from being frank with us." He turned again to Latimer. "All right, sir. If you didn't know, it is only natural that you should be upset. It's disappointing for us too. We've got to find her. I hoped she had said to you that she couldn't stick living at the Manor under present conditions, and you had offered to book a room for her at some hotel in Bath or Bristol or somewhere and run her over. Something like that. We shouldn't try to bring her back, you know, so long as we knew she was within reach. We try not to harass people more than we can help."

He had given Latimer time to recover. Latimer even essayed a smile as he answered, "All right. I'm prepared to agree that you mean well. I'm sorry I can't help you. I didn't know she was going, and I don't know where she's gone."

"Well, perhaps, just to round things off, you will tell me what you did yesterday from five o'clock until you returned to the hotel between twelve and one?"

"Certainly. I should explain that after I've been directing and acting I get very worked up. There's a lot of nerve strain about my job. You can't cover up mistakes. They come out on the screen. I'm best alone on these occasions. I go for a long walk or a run in my car to give myself a chance to simmer down. Yesterday I had no definite destination. I drove on aimlessly and eventually arrived in Taunton. I stopped at a pub there—I didn't notice the name. It was on the main street and had a yard where I left the car. I sat in the saloon bar until closing time. I got into the car and managed to get out of the town without running into anything, and then I drew up by the side of the road and slept for a bit. When I woke up I felt rather better and more able to drive. I got back somehow. I don't remember much about it."

"He'd had more than enough," said Evan. "I helped him upstairs and got him into bed."

"I see," said Collier. "Thank you, sir. I won't bother you any more now. I'll ask both you gentlemen to remain here for the present. It won't be more than a day or two. I hope."

"What about the rest of the unit?"

"We are arranging for them to stay on for another twenty-four hours." Collier thanked them again and withdrew.

There was a long silence. Then Latimer got up, moving slowly and heavily, like an old man, took a pocket flask of whisky out of his suitcase and poured some into his tooth-glass. "A couple of aspirin," he said, "washed down with this. Pain in my head. I ought not to drink. I haven't the physique for it. Why did you try to stop me just now?"

"I thought—I don't know," mumbled Evan. "I knew—at least, I guessed—that you'd got mixed up with her."

"We had an affair off and on all through the summer, when she came up to her sister's. I didn't take it seriously. After a while I began to be afraid that she did. It had lasted quite long enough. We talked it over—she had always known I'm not the marrying sort and that my work comes first. I thought she was going to be sensible. She told me about her husband's ambition to have a film made of the story he'd dug out of the family archives. It was really to please her that I agreed to come down here. She said that if we were to be just good friends in future we might make a start that way, and that she would always be so proud of having had a share in the making of one of my pictures. All that. I fell for it. We hadn't been in the house ten minutes when I saw what a mistake I had made. You remember how furious she was that I had brought you with me. She seemed to think I would be prepared to carry on the affair under her husband's roof. You remember she took me off the next day to see the ruined cottage in the woods. We had it out there. A violent quarrel, and then—well, I weakened, and I've regretted it ever since because it made her believe that the thing wasn't really over. Oh God, Bunny, a woman like that clings like a leech. I haven't seen her since, but she's written to me nearly every day. I haven't answered, but it's getting me down. I was terrified that she would turn up yesterday and make a row, claim the part of Vashti, go for Rosamund. She's mad and reckless enough for anything."

Evan gazed at him in horror. It was even worse than he had feared.

"When the story got hold of me, when I saw its possibilities, I was tempted more than once to risk everything and give her the part. She would have been the perfect Vashti. I've had to goad the Harper child into doing things that would have come naturally to Ida. I can just see her at the end, in that last shot we haven't taken yet, her wraith on the terrace of Great Baring, sated with her vengeance, laughing, with her hair streaming in the wind. But she was too insanely possessive, too utterly reckless. Poor old George was dense enough, but even his eyes would have been opened. There would have been a hell of a row and the picture would have been ruined."

"Did she—did she regard her husband as an obstacle?"

"I know what you're thinking," said Latimer drearily. "I can't believe it. She wasn't in love with him, never had been. She'd married for a home, for security. But he was devoted to her and did his best to give her anything she wanted. He bored her, but she was quite fond of him. She told me so."

"Have you any idea where she's gone, Stephen?"

"None. But I can imagine her rushing off when she felt she couldn't stand the Manor another minute. It would be quite in character. She'll be found staying at some hotel. It's very natural that she should want to get away from all the unpleasantness, if only for a day or two. I think the Arden girl should have waited a little longer. Why did she come to you, by the way?"

"I was able to help her about the old spaniel. She's been the under-dog at Little Baring. I suppose she realized I might have a fellow feeling for her."

Latimer, who had been glowering at the wall opposite, turned his head to look at his assistant director rather as if he were seeing him for the first time.

"You sound very bitter. Have you anything to complain off?"

"I think you might have told me all this earlier."

"What would have been the use? It's a rotten sort of thing to have to talk about. Let's stop now. That's the luncheon gong. We'd better go down, I suppose."

Evan was relieved to see that the Inspector and his colleague were not in the coffee-room. He ate mechanically and without appetite and noticed that Latimer hardly touched the food on his plate.

"What about a walk presently? There's a field way to Wookey."

Latimer agreed. It was as good a way as any of passing the time.

Evan had rung up Rosamund Harper at her hotel and she had told him she was spending the day in bed recovering from her exertions. "And I'm covered with bits of plaster and my right leg is bandaged. And if you tell me there'll be a re-take I shall burst into tears."

"O.K., Miss Harper. Don't worry. You were splendid. It's going to be the best thing Latimer has done. This picture will make film history." He hung up the receiver and joined Latimer, who was waiting for him in the hotel vestibule.

"Let's go and see the figures on the cathedral clock before we start on this walk. I haven't had a chance to look at them yet."

They were crossing the green towards the west door when young man came hurrying after them.

"Excuse me, sir, Inspector Collier would like a word with you."

"What? Again?"

"There have been fresh developments. I was sent to fetch you. I was told at the hotel that you had just gone out. This way, sir, if you'll come into the square. I left the car there."

Evan was prepared for an angry protest from Latimer, but he said nothing. They got into the back of the waiting car, and the young man who had followed them sat with the driver. During the drive Latimer smoked incessantly and looked out of the window. They passed through the village of Baring St. Mary and turned down the lane that skirted the pool, stopping by the gate that led into the Little Baring woods and the marshy valley in which the shots for the picture had been taken. Two other cars were drawn up in the lane with a couple of motor-cycles and several bicycles belonging to the lower ranks of the local constabulary.

Collier left a little group of men and came forward as the film director and his assistant got out of the car. His face was grave and his manner outer and more official than it had been.

"I have to tell you that Mrs. Condamine's car has been found. It had been left in a disused quarry just off the road between here and the village. Acting on information received, a close search was made of the ground here between the edge of the pool and the gate. The fragments of a letter were picked up and assembled. I have here a transcript of it.

'DARLING,

'You will have had the note I posted. Don't fail me. Meet me you know where when you've done work for the day. I shall wait for you. I have something to tell you, something that will make all the difference. You've been cruel, but I don't seem to mind. I'd rather be beaten by you than kissed by anyone else. I love you so frightfully.

'Your own Gipsy.'

"The envelope was addressed to Stephen Latimer, Esq. We have a witness, a village boy, who says Mrs. Condamine gave him a shilling to deliver this letter. He was not admitted to the field, but one of the extras offered to give it to the director and did so. The boy, watching through a gap in the hedge, saw you read it, tear it up and drop the pieces."

Latimer drew at his cigarette. "All right," he said harshly. "So what?"

"Did you comply with this very urgent summons and meet her?"

"No."

"Why not?"

"You're putting me in a damnably false position. This is a private matter."

"I'm afraid not now, Mr. Latimer."

"Very well. She had been writing to me every day. I had not answered her letters. I—I had finished. She—she was pestering me. That's the truth." He swallowed hard. "I know it makes me sound like a heel."

"Where is this meeting place, Mr. Latimer?"

"A ruined cottage up in the woods farther up the hill than the clearing where we've been working. She took me to see it when we first came down here. The tradition is that the witch who was drowned in this pool lived there, and she and Condamine thought it might come into the picture, but it's too far gone for that. We shall use a cottage built up in the studio."

"How often have you been up there?"

"Only once. The afternoon she showed it to me."

"We'll go there now. Will you lead the way?"

Latimer did not fall into the trap. "I don't know the way. We went to it from Little Baring. What about you, Evan?"

"I know," said Evan. "I took Sturt there, but he said it was too dark and overgrown."

"The invaluable Bunny," said Latimer, with a smile that did not reach his eyes. "It is the duty of every citizen to assist the police. Go with them, laddie. I'll wait for you here."

"I think you had better come with us, sir," said Collier firmly.

Latimer shrugged his shoulders and fell into step with Duffield. Collier went ahead with Evan, and three members of the local constabulary brought up the rear.

The marshy valley and wooded hillside that had been the scene of such intensive activity the previous day seemed almost uncannily silent and deserted now. Some of the reeds at the water's edge had been broken and trodden into the mire, and down by the gate there were prints of motor tyres in the muddy ground, and cigarette ends and empty cartons were scattered where technicians and extras had stood about, waiting.

In the clearing a scrap of red stuff caught on a thorn and torn from Rosamund Harper's skirt hung motionless in the windless autumn air.

So far no one had uttered a word. Evan broke the silence. "There's no actual path. We just went up the hill bearing a little to the left—"

They came, after a climb of about five minutes, to a much smaller open space shut in by trees and dense undergrowth. The four stone walls of the hovel stood, and a part of the chimney buried in ivy, but the thatched roof had fallen in long ago, and bracken, waist high, grew all round it and up to the threshold. There was no door. A mountain ash had sprung up within the enclosure between the blackened stones of what had once been the hearth. Ida

Condamine lay at the foot of the tree, face downwards. Her black hair was matted with dried blood and a cloud of flies rose from it, buzzing angrily, as Collier bent over her.

"One of you get back to Wells. Tell the Superintendent. A doctor and the ambulance. He'll know. All the doings. This is murder."

"Is she dead, sir?"

"Good God, yes. Stiff and cold. Look, Duffield, a spider has spun a web over her hand."

"Any sign of a weapon?"

"Here it is. A lump of limestone with blood and hair adhering. No help to us. There are stones like that lying about, hundreds of them. She must have struck the tree trunk as she fell. That would have stunned her. I wonder—" He raised his voice and said without looking round, "Mr. Latimer and Mr. Hughes. You will both remain here for the present."

Neither answered. Latimer had turned away and was being violently sick. Evan leant against the wall and was trying with shaking hands to strike a match for his cigarette. The two remaining policemen were pale and solemn.

The leaden minutes passed. Evan gave up trying to light his cigarette. He did not look at Latimer. He could hear the two men from the Yard moving about on the other side of the wall and talking in undertones. He shut his eyes. She was so lovely. Not kind, not safe to touch or to play with, but a lovely thing. He started violently and opened his eyes when Collier came out and spoke to him.

"This has been a shock for you. I won't detain you or Mr. Latimer any longer. You can go back to the hotel. I must ask you to remain there. I shall be seeing you again later. Benson, you can drive these gentlemen back to Wells."

Evan opened his mouth to speak and thought better of it. Latimer had already turned away and was wading through the sea of bracken clumsily as if he was not looking where he was going.

There was nobody in the hotel vestibule as they passed through. Latimer, who had not spoken before, said, "Come up to my room, Bunny. We'll have to talk about this."

Evan followed him reluctantly.

Latimer sat down heavily on the side of his bed. "Sit down—" He raised his weary blood-shot eyes slowly to his friend's face. "Why do you stand there by the door? I see. You think I killed her. Well, I can't blame you. All right, Bunny. Go away." Sighing, he leaned forward, resting his arms on his knees and staring vacantly at the worn carpet.

Evan, looking at him, felt an intolerable pang of pity. He moistened his dry lips. "Oh, Stephen, what madness—" He couldn't go on.

Latimer was not listening. "The picture. Only a miracle will save it now. If I'm arrested you must persuade the Studio to let you direct it. That will be the only way. You can do it. You know the thing from A to Z. We've worked on every scene together. Do your best for it, Bunny. It's meant a lot to me. My third—and tops. Why does a thing like this have to happen to me? What have I done to deserve it? It isn't a crime to have an affair with another man's wife. Anti-social, perhaps, but you aren't jailed for it. She was only amusing herself at first, just as I was. It's a risk one takes that the thing becomes an obsession. I can see that if she had persisted I might have killed her in the end. But I didn't. I didn't. God! My head's splitting. I can't think clearly. Look, Bunny. Go down, there's a good chap, and bring me a cup of tea, and leave me alone for a bit. I'll take some aspirin and lie down."

"That's a good idea, Stephen. You'll be better able to face up to things when you are rested," said Evan, trying to sound more confident than he felt.

He fetched the tea, and left Stephen lying on his bed in a darkened room. Weary as he was after the nervous strain of the past three days, he knew that he could not be easy until he had seen Lucy Arden.

A bus was just about to start as he came into the market square. He sat limply, as the heavy vehicle jolted along the now too familiar road to Baring St. Mary. His mind was in a painful turmoil. He was bound to Latimer by ties of long-standing affection and loyalty. He loved him as a man, and admired him as an artist. He was not blind to his faults, he knew that he was selfish, arrogant, unsparing of others. Anyone who stood in his way would be brushed aside. But—murder?

"I won't believe it," said Evan.

"Beg pardon?" said the old woman sitting next to him.

"Oh—nothing."

But—one must face facts—Stephen was being harassed and pursued by a woman he had ceased to love. There were historic crimes to prove the dangers of such cases. There was the affair of the Duc de Prasline, maddened by incessant scenes, letters, emotional demands, the interminable "I love you. Love me—" like drops wearing away the stone until the plaintive voice had to be silenced for ever. And, if Stephen did not kill her, who had? Someone had come to her as she waited in that ruined cottage—waited, admittedly, for Stephen. Who else could have known she would be there? Who else had a motive?

He got out at the cross-roads and turned in between the stone gate-posts to trudge up the long avenue to the house that loomed darkly, with unlit windows, in the gathering dusk.

Chapter XII
A DOUBT REMAINS

Evan turned the handle, but the door was locked.

He rang the bell and waited. After what seemed a long time he heard slow uncertain footsteps, and a voice said, "Who is it?"

"It's me, Evan Hughes."

Bolts were drawn and the key turned. As the door was opened he saw Lucy's pale face seeming to hang disembodied and nearly on a level with his own against the darkness within. What happened next was unplanned. Evan found himself holding her inexpertly, but with considerable firmness, in his arms, with sensations that were definitely new to him and, on the whole, agreeable.

"Oh," Lucy murmured, "I've been so frightened. I'm so glad you've come—"

"Darling." He added incoherently and irrationally, "You'll be all right now."

"Yes. The Inspector came just now and told me about Ida. It's so awful. But he was very kind. He was going to telephone to the police in Taunton to see if Mrs. Trask can't come back, and if she can they'll bring her over themselves, so I shan't be alone. Mrs. Trask is a good sort. She and I get on. Oh, Evan, this must be frightful for you. A person you've looked up to and been fond of."

"If you mean Latimer," he said, "he didn't do it. Look, Lucy, I'm tired and hungry. Let's light a lamp and have some kind of a meal."

"Yes, of course," she said more cheerfully. "You poor thing. Come into the kitchen. I've got a fire there and a kettle on. We'll have tea and poached eggs on toast."

"Fine. But first—" he fumbled with a clumsy gentleness for her chin, turned her face up and kissed her. There was no doubt at all about her response. She took his hand and led him through the dark hall and down the stone-paved passage to the kitchen where there was lamplight and firelight, and he sat down in the shabby armchair while she ran about, flushed and bright-eyed, making toast and poaching eggs.

"I love you, Lucy. Will you marry me?"

"Of course. If you're sure you really want me. It's so marvellous that you should. I'm not a bit glamorous or anything."

"I don't like glamour. It's all right on the screen, of course. Gosh! I'm happy just sitting here and having high tea with you. That's queer, isn't it, in the midst of all that has happened and is going to happen. It's like being in the stillness in the centre of the whirlwind."

"I feel the same. Let's just try not to think of anything but you and me until—until we have to."

"When do you expect Mrs. Trask to arrive?"

"The Inspector said they would bring her or some other woman to keep me company by nine o'clock if not sooner. Until then he told me to lock all the doors and let no one in."

"I wonder why he did that," said Evan thoughtfully. Perhaps, after all, Collier was not entirely convinced of Latimer's guilt. After all, it was possible that Ida Condamine had been killed by a homicidal maniac. How could they be sure that among the sixty film extras and the fourteen technicians they had brought down there was not one mentally unbalanced? There must have been opportunities for many of them to wander away into the woods unnoticed while scenes in which they were not taking part were being shot. Or it might have been some local half-wit. In that case Collier's evident anxiety was justified. Lucy might be in danger alone at the Manor with a killer at large.

"I shall stay here until someone turns up."

The night had turned chilly. They built up the fire and Lucy sat on a stool, leaning against his knees, while the white-faced clock on the dresser ticked away the peaceful minutes.

They spoke very little. There would be time enough later to make plans. "I shall be leaving here," she said. "The Inspector said he would find lodgings for me in Wells. Cousin Julia wants to move in here with Ozzie as soon as possible."

At a quarter to nine they heard a car and the front door bell was rung. Lucy lit a candle and they went to the door together, but Evan stood back unnoticed while Mrs. Trask came in and folded the girl in a large embrace.

"What you've been through, dearie. 'Tes a shame—"

Evan joined the policeman on the doorstep. "Can you give me a lift back to Wells?"

"That'll be all right, sir." He raised his voice. "I'll be leaving you now, ma'am. Reckon you'll take care of the young lady."

"She'll be safe along of I, Tom Puddock. Good night to 'ee."

"She seems to know you," said Evan as he got in beside the driver.

"Ar. She's my wife's sister. My wife was brought up to Baring St. Mary. 'Tes a queer place seemingly. Her always said so. Full of ghostesses, what with beasts coming down from the church roof and her that walks up to Great Baring and her hair blowing like smoke in the gale 'tesn't a place to be out alone by night." Constable Puddock slowed down and sounded his horn as they came out into the road, and added rather hastily, "'Tes only old tales and ignorance."

They were passing through the village. The stream creeping along the house walls under the tumbledown plank bridges reflected the stars with a glaucous gleam. The cottages seemed to be sinking under innumerable layers of rotting thatch. A dim light flickered here and there through diamond panes. There was a ground mist, and Evan thought he caught a whiff of the faint sickly smell he had noticed when he walked through the place.

Puddock set his passenger down in the market square when they reached Wells, and drove on to the police station.

Evan decided that it would be only right to look in on Rosamund Harper. He would not admit even to himself that he shrank from spending the rest of the evening with Latimer.

He found Rosamund sitting in the lounge of her hotel with Sturt. They both seemed glad to see him.

"What's going on here? The place is full of rumours, but no one tells us anything. The cops have been here but all they said was that we were to stay put until further notice," said Sturt.

Rosamund was staring at their assistant director. "Gosh. You look like something the cat brought in," she said with her usual devastating candour.

"That's how I feel, darling."

"Ring the bell, Sturt, he must have a drink. Tell us, is it true that there's been another murder?"

"Yes. Mrs. Condamine. She was found up in the woods with her head battered in."

"When?"

"This afternoon. But they think it happened yesterday."

"Those woods where we were working?"

"Yes."

Rosamund frowned. "Not so good. Do you think it can have anything to do with our lot? I mean, this crime wave rather coincides with our arrival on the scene. Is it just a coincidence? As advance publicity, it isn't what I would have chosen."

Rosamund had been an extra herself not so long ago. As an actress she was malleable, which is a quality that appeals to directors, and she had realized Latimer's conception of Vashti with a thoroughness that had seemed likely to assure her future. Probably she already saw herself in her dreams with a bungalow in Beverley Hills, complete with grounds and a swimming pool. Latimer, in picking her out from among several candidates, had been influenced by her superficial likeness to Ida Condamine, but though her small dusky face photographed well, she was not really pretty. She was, however, extremely intelligent, which, in the end, is often better.

Evan drank his whisky. "It will all be cleared up in a day or two. The police are doing their stuff."

Not far away, in the Superintendent's room at the police station, a consultation was in progress. The Chief Constable was present and had listened closely to Collier's report of the latest developments.

"It seems to me that you've got it in the bag," he said. "Mrs. Condamine's infatuation for this film director fellow provides the motive. She poisoned her husband, hoping that her lover would marry her, but he turned her down. There was a quarrel when he met her in the woods, and she resorted to threats or blackmail, and he saw red as men are apt to in such cases."

"It might be," said Collier slowly, "but I believe the medical evidence will prove that she was attacked by someone who came up behind her and took her unawares. The light was failing when we found her and we are making an intensive search of the spot to-morrow which may give us further indications."

"He may have left her and come back."

"If he committed the crime it must have been between about twenty-past four when the last members of the film unit left the ground and about seven. His story of spending most of the evening drinking in the bar of a pub in Taunton is true. We rang up the police there to help us and within the hour they had traced his movements. The barmaid in the saloon bar of the Three Ducks recognized him from the description. Age about thirty, above the average height. Very thick chestnut-coloured hair worn rather long, regular features, red-brown eyes, rusty-red pullover, brown tweed sports coat, and brown corduroy slacks. She noticed him particularly—most women do, I fancy—though he hardly spoke to her. He seemed gloomy and was drinking steadily. She thought he might have been let down by some girl."

"That's no alibi. There would be plenty of time between half-past four and seven. How does he account for it?"

"He says he drove about aimlessly for a while and pulled up by the roadside for a bit."

"Not very convincing."

"No."

"It's a bad business," said the Chief Constable. "The Condamines are a very old family and at one time they owned a lot of land. Latterly, of course, they've come down in the world. Condamine's great grandfather was a gambler. They have had no money for repairs. They and their tenants have taken all they could get from the land and put nothing back. You've seen the village. No drainage, nothing."

"No great catch being the heir then," said Collier thoughtfully.

"Very little in it, I imagine." The Chief Constable cleared his throat. "Now—I don't want to butt in. The Yard are in charge. But I confess I'm rather surprised that you aren't making an arrest to-night."

Collier was doodling on a piece of blotting paper, rows of question marks. "I like to be sure," he said.

"And aren't you? Isn't that note he tore up damning enough?"

Collier agreed, but he looked unhappy. "He strikes me as the sort of man who shirks unpleasantness. According to him he wanted to have done with a complicated emotional tangle and give all his time and energy to his work, which means more to him than any woman, and with that end in view he was ignoring her letters and keeping out of her way. You can call that heartless and callous if you like, but it's understandable. The circumstances of her death, the savagery of the attack, give me the feeling that there is more to it than we yet know. It may sound odd, but I should be happier about it if she'd been strangled. If, in the course of a bitter quarrel she had said something that so infuriated him that he took her by the throat—"

"I see," said the Chief Constable unexpectedly, "you feel that there's something wrong with the psychological set-up."

"Exactly. It's like a picture I was looking at the other day. There seemed to be something phoney about it, and after a while I realized what it was. A sail at sea was filled by the wind, but the draperies of the women standing on the shore were being blown in the opposite direction."

"But someone killed her, and in the way you object to," said the Chief Constable. "Who else is there?"

"The doctor said that in his opinion she had been dead at least twenty-four hours when we found her this afternoon, and he declined to commit himself further than that. We have been assuming that she was killed round about the time when she expected Latimer to meet her, but she may have left and returned later. In the case of George Condamine we had a list of six suspects, Ida Condamine, Lucy Arden, Mrs. Luke Condamine and her son Oswald, the rector, and the unknown whom we usually write down as X. There might be somebody in this list who, having committed one murder, found it necessary, for security reasons, to kill again."

No one spoke for a minute. They were all impressed by Collier's evident anxiety.

Collier resumed. "The case against Latimer is strong, but I want it to be fool-proof before I move, and not only for my own sake. I don't much like what I've seen of him. I should say he was a complete egoist—and most murderers are that, damned sorry for themselves and without a grain of pity for their victims—but, on the other hand, the people who work with him seem to think very highly of him, and that little Welshman, his secretary, is devoted to him; and, if you happen to take the art of making films seriously, you'll know that he's valuable. People who understand these matters say he's a genius in his own line."

"Genius or not," said the Chief Constable bluntly, "if he's put in dock and a jury finds him guilty he'll hang."

"I know. I know. But meanwhile he's not an old lag who can be detained for questioning and allowed to go a few hours later none the worse for the experience."

"Very well, Inspector. But if he gets away you will be responsible."

"I don't think he will, sir. I wouldn't trust his common sense. He might bolt like a frightened horse. But his friend has got his head screwed on the right way and won't let him make a fool of himself."

The Chief Constable pushed back his chair. "That's settled then. Unless you get fresh instructions in the morning from the Yard you'll carry on with this enquiry as a part of your case, and we'll do all we can to help."

"Thank you, sir. You've been very good so far."

They shook hands. The Chief Constable went out to his car, and Collier and Duffield walked back through the moonlit streets to their hotel.

Collier was depressed. "I never liked this job," he said. "I like it less than ever now."

"You're too soft-hearted. That's your trouble," remarked the sergeant. "You've been standing up for Latimer, but you think him guilty, and you wish he wasn't."

Collier sighed. "Sarge, you read me like a book."

CHAPTER XIII
REACTIONS AMONG SUSPECTS

"WAKE up, darling."

Oswald Condamine blinked sleepily at his mother, standing by his bedside with his breakfast-tray.

"You're up with the lark, that overrated bird."

"Nonsense. Sit up. I've lots to do."

Julia Condamine was an early riser, and her son was not. During the summer she was often up by six o'clock and working in the room she called her studio. She was so spare and active, so excitable and impulsive, and he so fat and flabby and torpid that the contrast between them was almost ludicrous. Ida Condamine had once compared them to a grasshopper and a slug, and George had laughed and said, "You've got it exactly," before he bethought himself and added, "My dear, that's not very kind."

Oswald sat up, still grumbling, and arranged the pillows behind his back while his mother drew the blinds, placed the bed table in position with the tray on it, and poured out a cup of coffee.

"All right," he said irritably, "I can help myself. I'm not a baby."

"Yes you are, duckie. My baby." The gay, brittle voice with its trick of over-emphasis that reminded listeners of those letters in which every other word is heavily underlined and every other sentence rounded off with exclamation marks, clacked on as she moved about the room, folding clothes, shutting a drawer left half-open. Oswald was used to it and, in any case, did not suffer from nerves. He went on stolidly eating his bacon and eggs and munching toast while she talked.

"Lots to do. I'm going over to the Manor now to have it out with Lucy. She's a sticker, and if I'm not firm she'll go on living there at our expense. She should be satisfied with having cajoled poor George into leaving her that absurdly large legacy. Most uncalled for. Injudicious really. People will be wondering what she did to earn it. I meant to run over yesterday evening, but my torch battery has given out, and I couldn't find yours."

"There was a moon."

"Yes. But even with a moon it's dark going through the woods."

She was standing with her back to him looking out of the window at the tiny front garden screened from the road by an overgrown hedge. "Ozzie, you left your motor-cycle out all night. You must have come home very late."

He grinned. "Round about two-ish. Didn't you hear me?"

"No. I'd taken some of that stuff the doctor prescribed last year. I haven't been sleeping well since—I can't help worrying—"

"Shouldn't worry," he said, not unkindly. "After all, it's coming out not so badly for us, especially if you're right, as I expect you are, about that picture in the dining-room. It's lucky neither George or Ida realized its value and that he left me the house and its contents."

"Ozzie, will it be all right now about that firm that has been bothering you?"

"Quite all right. I've been in touch with them. They were very stiff, but agreed to wait for the money."

"Good. Well, I must be off—"

She had nearly reached the door when he said, "What about Ida? Are you pushing her out too? It won't look very well, you know."

She stopped abruptly. "Ozzie! Don't you know? But, of course, how should you. You were out all day and didn't come home until late. She's dead. Her body was found up in the woods. That detective from London came and told me. It was a most awful shock, of course."

The fat, white face turned towards her was expressionless as a lump of putty. "Murdered?"

"Yes."

"Who did it? Do they suspect anyone? Did he say?"

"He didn't say much, but from the questions he asked I was able to make a pretty good guess. I went with Lucy to the pool to watch them shooting some of the scenes for the film, with that Miss Harper taking the part Ida wanted. I happened to notice that Mr. Latimer received some sort of note or message while he was standing near the gate talking to the camera-men. He read it and tore it up at once. One of the extras gave it him, but he had it from a boy who was not allowed to come in. I saw who it was. Young Benny Samways who does odd jobs at the Manor when he wants to earn a few pence. I put two and two together, and when I told the Inspector about it I think he did the same."

"I don't get it."

"Nonsense, Ozzie, you're not as dense as all that. Ida and her trips to Town. She'd been carrying on with Mr. Latimer and that's why he came down here in the first place. She was mad about him and didn't take much trouble to hide it. If poor George hadn't been so soft about her—and as blind as a bat. She made a dead set at Mallory at one time. I don't know how far that went. The rector may be a saint, but, if you ask me, he's got a poker face and can play a poker hand. Well, the lovely Ida played with fire, and she got burned. You'll see. The next thing you'll see in the papers will be 'West country murder mystery. Arrest of famous film director.'"

"Well, don't have a row with Lucy, Mother. Rows are a mistake. And too much talking."

She looked at him oddly for a moment before she said, "I dare say you're right," and went out, closing the door carefully.

At five minutes to eight the Reverend Sebastian Mallory left the Rectory and crossed the churchyard where the flowers had withered on the mound of raw yellow clay that was George Condamine's grave, to the vestry door. One of the peal of bells clanged uncertainly twice and relapsed into silence. Mallory was bell-ringer as well as celebrant on these occasions and he did not expect to see any congregation, though occasionally Lucy Arden was there, kneeling in the Little Baring pew. She was there this morning. He noticed her as he went up to the altar and waited for her to make the responses. When the service was over and he came out of the vestry in his old black cassock she was in the porch.

"Lucy, my dear—"

"You've heard?"

"Just now, before I came out. My housekeeper had it from the boy who brings the milk. It's all over the village. Terrible. Ida. So lovely. Have they found the man?"

"What did they tell you?"

"That Ida was set upon by one of these people who have been brought down from London to take part in this film business. How I wish now that I had tried to dissuade George from this picture business."

"You sound like Millie Trask. She thinks that raking up the old story has revived the curse the gipsy laid on the Condamines. Mr. Mallory, is it true that she's buried by the north wall of the church and that Hugh Condamine and one of his servants dug the grave after dark because the sexton wouldn't do it, and read the burial service, and that until the end of his life he used to put flowers on it, but they were always blown away by the wind?"

"My dear child, how should I know? Did George read that in those old letters and diaries he was always poring over?"

"Yes. He used to tell me, because no one else was really interested. He had got so wrapped up in the story. It was a kind of obsession. He didn't say much so nobody knew how often he wasn't here at all but living through things that happened three hundred years ago. I think he had almost persuaded himself to believe that he and Ida were reincarnations of Hugh and Vashti. It was a sort of compensation—I think that's what the psycho-analysts call it—because he knew that Ida didn't care much for him, but Vashti, in her primitive way, simply worshipped Hugh."

The rector had listened with growing interest. He had always liked Lucy and felt rather sorry for her, thinking that she was put upon and bullied by her relations. He was unprepared for this shrewd summing up of George's mentality.

"Dear me," he said, "a chiel amang us taking notes. I had no idea. Lookers-on see most of the game, eh?" He broke off in some confusion, feeling vaguely that he had said the wrong thing.

Lucy answered calmly, "Yes. I was always an onlooker at Little Baring. Sometimes I felt it was hard as I was the youngest person there. Twenty-two, and a back number."

"Why did you stay on? I sometimes wondered when Ida was being difficult."

"I was fond of George. Two years ago I would have married him if he had asked me. But he went off for a holiday and met Ida. So that was that. I soon saw that I must remain and look after things if he was to have any comfort. Ida thought of nothing but her own clothes. She was as useless as a little cat. More useless. She didn't catch mice."

"Hush, Lucy, for God's sake. She's dead."

She looked at him with a faint smile. "Have I shocked you? Is it news to you that I hated her, not so much for trampling on me as for the way she treated George?"

"Yes. Yes, I see," he said feebly.

"And that isn't all. You know how he died—after hours of suffering, poisoned by the sandwiches I cut for them. She must have arranged that so that I should be suspected. She told me where they had their lunch on the way up Crookes Peak. I know the place, a slope of smooth turf and a glorious view across the Channel to the Welsh mountains. I've thought and thought, and imagined her sitting by him, watching him while he ate. I—"

She burst into tears.

"My poor child," said Mallory, adding, "Here, take mine," as she fumbled for her handkerchief. "This has all been too much for you. Will you stop and have breakfast with me?"

"No, thanks, I must get back. Thank you for being kind."

Lucy walked back to the Manor. She would be alone throughout the day, for Mrs. Trask's daughter was still on the danger list and she had been promised a lift to and from Taunton.

"I'll be back before nightfall, dearie," she had said, "and we'll have a bit of supper together."

It was not much after nine, but there had already been one visitor. Mrs. Luke had called and had dropped an old envelope through the letter-box, with a message scrawled in pencil on the back.

"Knocked and rang but couldn't make you hear. Will come again later. Please get on with your packing. J.C."

Lucy's lips were pressed together as she read it. Why was Cousin Julia in such a hurry to push her out? She must know that she had very little ready money and nowhere to go. She went into the kitchen where Mrs. Trask had lit the fire and left the kettle on the stove. The silence of the house was oppressive. She found herself listening, straining to hear. Such a little while ago there would have been so many normal familiar sounds. Mrs. Trask working the carpet sweeper, Punch pattering up and down stairs after George; and voices, the voice of Ida, languid and discontented: "Lucy, have you mended that ladder in my stocking? Oh, damn, Where's the vanishing cream?" George, humming to himself, a little off key, his favourite tune "Lord Rendal", or calling for her: "Lucy, is this your shopping morning? Get me some more baccy, that's a good girl—"

She made some toast and sat down to have her breakfast in the kitchen. Why had she talked like that to Mr. Mallory? He had been kind, but she felt that she had antagonized him. He could not understand. He had been half in love with Ida Condamine. It showed sometimes, though not often, in his face when he looked at her. He had conquered his weakness long ago, but it had left him with a soft spot where she was concerned. Punch. If they had let her keep Punch she would not be afraid to be alone in the house. But he was safe at the vet's. Safe.

Collier and Duffield had nearly finished their breakfast when Evan Hughes came into the dining-room. He wished them good morning as he edged his way round their table, and Collier took the opportunity to speak to him.

"How is your friend this morning?"

"He had a bad night as you might expect. He's sleeping now."

"And yours wasn't too good," said Collier sympathetically.

"He wanted to talk, and the least I could do was to listen. We're friends, you know. He's been a good friend to me. He got me this job. He's not the—the person you're looking for, Inspector. I'm absolutely convinced of that."

"Appearances are against him."

"I know." He looked anxiously at Collier. "You—you aren't going to arrest him—"

"I shall be taking a risk if I don't, but—I will be frank with you, Hughes. I'm not entirely convinced of his guilt. I'll wait another twenty-four hours—on one condition."

"What is that?"

They were talking in lowered voices, ignoring the curious glances and whispers of fellow guests breakfasting in the farther end of the long room.

"That you will stay with him and see to it that he does not do anything foolish."

Evan's face changed slightly. They could see that it was not a welcome assignment. But he answered firmly, "Very well."

"I rely on you, mind. If anything goes wrong I shall be blamed, not you. I'm making you responsible, but actually the responsibility will be mine. If you let me down I shall be sunk."

Evan nodded. "I understand. I'll do my best. I can't say more." He was thinking, "I was going to see Lucy. That'll have to wait until to-morrow. This chap is right. If Stephen's goaded he might do any fool thing."

He passed on to his table, and Collier and his companion rose and strolled out, pausing in the vestibule to tap the barometer. When they were outside and crossing the street Duffield said, "What's the big idea? It must be him. Why don't you want to pull him in?"

"Just a hunch. I can't see him meeting a woman if he didn't want to. On the other hand, if he's over-driven he'll go off the rails. Oodles of talent and very little common sense. If I'm not mistaken that little Welshman supplies the ballast in the combination."

"Poor little devil," said the placid Duffield commiseratingly. "He looks like death warmed up this morning. I doubt if he's as convinced of his friend's innocence as he tried to make out."

They turned into the police station. Several reports had come in from various sources and had been taken down and neatly typed by a fresh-faced and ingenuous-looking youth lately promoted from the uniformed branch and placed at the disposal of the visitors from the Yard. The Superintendent was out, but hoped they would make use of his room.

Collier sat down and filled and lit his pipe before he settled down to work. "What's your name?"

"Grinstead, sir, Harold Grinstead."

"Local?"

"My people live in Weston."

"Can you drive a car?"

"Yes, sir."

"Good. I'd be glad if you could drive us to-day. I usually drive myself, but I've a good deal on my mind. But first we'll just run through these. Sebastian Mallory, priest, unmarried. Twenty years incumbent of Baring St. Mary. He was three years previous to that in an East End curacy and took country living after a severe nervous breakdown. Entered the church by way of a theological college, having previously studied medicine but without passing his final exams. That's rather interesting, Duffield. While a medical student was charged with violently assaulting husband of one of the hospital's out-patients, but was discharged and congratulated by the magistrate after the hearing of the evidence which showed that the complainant had knocked his wife down and kicked her, narrowly missing the month-old baby she was carrying in her arms."

Duffield beamed. "That's the ticket."

Collier laid the report down. He said nothing. Duffield glanced at him and his smile faded.

"Lucy Arden, educated at a school for the daughters of clergymen. On leaving school went home to assist her widowed mother, who kept a small and unsuccessful boarding house. Her mother died during the war, and Lucy entered the land army, strained her back and was invalided out. She worked for a while as a dispenser. She was then offered a home by a distant relative, George Condamine, and has lived at Little Baring ever since."

"Well, that's harmless," said Duffield.

"Ida Condamine. Was engaged as a receptionist and entertainer at the Hotel Superbia at Bournemouth during the summer of 1945, but left at the end of three months to marry George Condamine, who had met her there. The manageress remembers her well and says the gentlemen found her attractive but that she did not take any trouble to carry out her duties and totally ignored the lady visitors. She had been given notice when she became engaged to Mr. Condamine. The references she gave when she applied for the post have not been preserved, and so far nothing more is known of her antecedents. Her maiden name was Beverly, which might be phoney."

"There's her married sister in London," said Duffield.

"Yes. But her husband has been sent out to the Melbourne branch of his firm, and they are on their way out now. They must be thanking their stars they got away just in time to escape being mixed up in a murder case. The next on our list is Mrs. Luke Condamine. Nothing known about her previous to her marriage which took place twenty-five years ago. After her husband's death she and her boy made their home at Little Baring until George married. Since then she has lived, rent free, in a cottage half a mile down the road. No evidence of any quarrel or unpleasantness. She appeared to be on friendly terms with George and his wife and was often in and out. Sketches in water colours and often refers to her art-student days.

"At first sight she seems to gain from George's death since her son gets the bulk of the estate, but according to Mr. Rand there will be very little to live on when the legacies have been paid out and the death duties. He seems to think the benefits are illusory and that she is quite sharp enough to know it."

"What about the son?"

"He's a more promising subject. Do you know anything about him, Grinstead?"

"He hasn't a very good name locally, sir. He's had several jobs, but never stays long anywhere. Very unsatisfactory. His mother won't hear a word against him. She says he's delicate. Fact is, he's bone lazy."

"Has he ever been in actual trouble with the police?"

"No, sir. There have been some nasty rumours at times. Something about him torturing cats. But there was nothing to take hold of and it may not be true. The Condamines have a name for being queer. It's an old family, sir, and it's said they intermarried a lot."

"Just so. I see here that his last employers were Caston and Butts, turf accountants, with an address at Weston. Do you know anything about them?"

Collier was amused to see young Grinstead blush like a girl. Perhaps he was an occasional client of the firm.

"Quite reliable people, sir. A well-conducted business. Nothing against them."

"Good. We'll call on them and get the low-down on Master Ozzie. We're going to Weston anyhow."

Ten minutes later the smart dark-blue police car was away on the road to Axbridge, with Grinstead, bolt upright and very official and poker-faced, at the wheel. Collier sat by him, his grey eyes remote and unseeing, immersed in his thoughts.

Nothing, really, in those dossiers. A double murder, with a time lag. One person might have committed both crimes, but it didn't really follow. Say that Ida was the poisoner. She had a motive since she was in love with Latimer. That, at any rate, was an undisputed fact. Who, then, killed her, and why? Was her death tied to the murder of her husband, or was there no connection? Two murders in the same family within a week, and unconnected? No. One couldn't swallow that. And yet—there was the presence in and near those woods, during that day, of all those film extras brought down from London for the making of the picture. Most of them, no doubt, respectable hardworking people, but among them, possibly, if not probably, more than one denizen of the underworld. The attack might have been unpremeditated, the attacker might not have meant to kill. Mrs. Condamine had been wearing a diamond engagement ring, a gold wrist-watch. She had not been robbed, but it might be that the attacker had lost his nerve when he realized what he had done.

The more he thought of it the more likely it seemed that this was the solution. The thing might have happened earlier than they had assumed at first. The film crowd had been milling about there from eight o'clock onwards, and any one of them might have wandered off unnoticed at some time or other. He must remember to ask the doctor if she might not have been dead longer than they thought. He was probably doing the post-mortem now. He had rung up to say that he had been delayed, having been called out to a maternity case.

He might have hit on the truth. After all, coincidences might happen, though he couldn't imagine this one being very well received by his superiors at the Yard. But was he any nearer getting his man?

CHAPTER XIV
THE INVESTIGATION CONTINUES

THEY were getting in to Weston now. Grinstead drew up before a new block of shops and offices. "Caston and Butts have their office on the first floor over the fishmongers."

Collier got out, followed by Duffield, and they went in after telling Grinstead to wait. The name of the firm was on a brass plate by the side door, and a steep flight of stairs led up to the turf accountants' premises. The synthetic blonde seated at the typewriter in the ante-room rose very promptly as they entered. "Yes, sir?"

"Mr. Caston or Mr. Butts?"

"Mr. Caston will see you if you will come this way." They exchanged glances. Evidently Mr. Caston and his staff had seen them getting out of the police car. The secretary, obviously, had forgotten some of her lines. She should have asked their names and gone through the routine of finding out if her employer was disengaged. She was young and had the rather flashy doll-like prettiness of her type. Collier spoke just as she was about to open the inner door.

"Just a minute. Were you working in this office when young Condamine was employed here?"

Her colour faded, leaving two patches of rouge on her cheekbones.

"I—yes—why?"

"Don't be frightened," he said gently. "No need for that. Have you seen him lately?"

"Do I have to answer?"

"No. But it might be the best thing all round if you did."

"No." She was defiant now. "I have nothing to say."

"Very well. Think it over. I may be seeing you again later."

She opened the door and stood back to let them pass in.

Mr. Caston was a spruce, youngish man with a genial manner. He greeted them as if they were his most valued customers and offered cigarettes. "Take a pew. A light. Allow me. Now, gentlemen, what can I do for you?"

"You are young Condamine's most recent employers."

"Yes," said Mr. Caston dryly. "I suppose we may be. What of it?"

"You sacked him?"

"I wouldn't put it so brutally. He was unsuited to an office life. He was not fitted by temperament to be one of the world's workers. That is all that need be said."

"I suppose that a certain amount of money would have passed through his hands?" suggested Collier, and noted a just perceptible reaction to the operative words. It was just a slight twitch of the facial muscles, but it sufficed to show him he was on the right track.

"Naturally," said Mr. Caston, after a pause that had been a little too long. "You know what our business is. Gee-gees. We run it on the level. Definitely. We have nothing to complain of, and we don't anticipate any trouble from any direction. Is that good enough?"

He smiled disarmingly and Collier smiled back at him. He rather liked Mr. Caston.

"Any little irregularity will be put right now, or as soon as funds are available, I suppose?"

Caston said nothing for a minute. He looked at Collier steadily. The hard core under the surface geniality was very apparent now.

"I believe in everyone minding their own business. And that goes for the police, too."

"Oh, quite. But a murder has been committed, Mr. Caston, as you must have heard, I think. Young Condamine will gain something—not very much, but something— through his uncle's death."

"You don't infer—" Caston seemed quite genuinely shocked. "How very unpleasant. No, Inspector, it couldn't be. Young Condamine spent that day in Weston. I saw him myself lunching at the Cadena, and later on the sands. He spends a lot of his time here. I'll be frank and admit that he's a good-for-nothing waster, but a murderer—oh, no. I can't, I won't believe it."

"You are reading far too much into a simple remark," said Collier mildly. "We just thought it would be interesting to find out if he was, in any way, pressed for money. Not that he'll get much."

"Why do you say that? There's the 'Constable'. But you probably wouldn't know about that."

"What constable?" Collier was puzzled.

Caston eyed him thoughtfully, evidently weighing the benefits that might accrue to him from having helped the police against the advantages of remaining aloof, and coming down on the side of co-operation with the authorities.

"Well, I only know what young Oswald told me. The Baring property is entailed. The land isn't worth much and the house is out of repair and needs hundreds spent on it, but the contents of the house go with the entail, and there is one thing, which his uncle did not know about, which is going to make all the difference."

"What is it?"

"It seems that there are several more or less dingy old pictures in heavy gilt frames hanging on the walls. They've been there for donkey's years, and no one notices them any more than you'd notice die fire irons or the umbrella stand. Now Ozzie's great grandmother came from Suffolk, and one of her wedding presents was a picture by a local artist, which was put in a dark corner of the dining-room where it has been ever since. I know nothing about art, so I just said, 'So what?' He said that his mother, who went in for art and all that before she married, said it was a 'Constable'. Well, I still wasn't impressed, but I could see he believed it really was worth something, so I started a few enquiries here and there about this 'Constable' and the prices his pictures fetched. I don't mind telling you it took my breath away. Ten thousand, twenty thousand.

Just a bit of canvas with paint smeared over it. I mean to say! But it's a fact."

"And his uncle didn't realize that he was the possessor of this treasure?"

"No."

"I see," said Collier very thoughtfully. "Thanks very much, Mr. Caston. You have been very helpful. This may or may not be important. It must not go any further. I can rely on you for that?"

"You can. It may all be a fairy-tale. It's only what he told me."

"But if it's true, he's sitting pretty. Just so. Well, we won't take up any more of your time."

As they went out, the blonde typist was engaged on facial repairs.

"Hands shaking," remarked Duffield as they went down the stairs.

"I noticed it."

The hotel whose annex had been booked for the film people was only a hundred yards farther down the road. Collier told Grinstead to take the car on to the sea front and wait for them there. He wanted to discuss what they had learned from the turf accountant with Duffield.

"Nice to get a whiff of sea air," said the sergeant placidly as they walked on together.

"Very. He was lying part of the time, of course."

"Crooked?" said the sergeant doubtfully.

"Not exactly. No. Just a case of *suppressio vert* in the interests of a previous arrangement. He was only trying to be fair to the other party in the deal. You can't blame him for that. My guess is that he caught young Condamine out in some peculations, cooking the books or what not. There was a show-down, and he agreed not to prosecute if Condamine would pay back in full. That accounts, as nothing else would, for his knowing all about the Constable. Ozzie told him to prove he had expectations. No harm in that, but it created a dangerous situation. It gives young Condamine a pretty strong motive for getting rid of his uncle, but makes it even less likely than before that he committed the second murder."

"How's that?"

"He might have disliked the thought of paying the widow her life interest if that meant leaving him practically as penniless as before, but the Constable would change all that."

"Could it really be worth as much as Caston said?"

"Probably more."

Sturt was waiting for them at the door of the hotel annex. "We've got them rounded up for you," he said, "in the room the management lets out for bean feasts. Will you see the small-part people first? They rather expect preferential treatment."

"Very well."

"You can see them in the writing-room." He opened a door and ushered them in. "Here you are. We've had instructions from the Studios that we are to assist the police in every possible way. Anything more I can do?"

"You know what we're trying to get at?"

"Not exactly. No."

Sturt was wearing what seemed to be almost a uniform for the film unit: corduroy slacks, very baggy at the knees and stained with chemicals, and a soiled woollen pullover. In spite of his casual manner, Collier got the impression that he was very much on his guard.

"It is quite simple. Your people were employed at intervals throughout the day before yesterday within a quarter of a mile of the spot where a woman was subsequently found murdered. Most of them, I daresay, were never out of the sight of friends or acquaintances who can vouch for them, and be vouched for in turn. Others, who cannot produce an alibi, will have to give a detailed account of their movements while they were not actually acting under Mr. Latimer's direction. Incidentally, we shall be taking everybody's finger-prints."

"O.K. But I think you'll find that there was little or no wandering away into the woods. We had rigged up two of the usual offices, one for men and one for women not far from the field gate, and our mobile canteen was there supplying tea, coffee and buns. You can take it from me that when people weren't acting they were watching the others being put through it by Latimer. It's fascinating to watch, and they're all pretty keen."

"It has to be done," said Collier.

Nearly three hours later he had to admit that Sturt was right. All his victims seemed perfectly ready and even eager to answer any questions regarding the day before yesterday, though a few were inclined to be rather cagey about their past. Everybody's attention had been fixed on what went on before the cameras. The youngest was a girl of fourteen, the eldest a man of seventy-five, who had been a member of Irving's company at the Lyceum in the 'nineties. "I used to look down on the cinema and trot out cheap sneers about celluloid emotion, and I only tried for work at film studios because a man must eat," he said. "But Stephen Latimer, sir, is a genius. He's got personality, drive, imagination. Damme, sir, I feel it an honour to work under him, and I haven't felt like that under any management since Sir Henry died. I am sorry," said the old actor largely, "I am grieved for the poor lady who, we are told, was done to death in those woods while we were enacting a tragedy of three centuries ago, but I believe that if a massacre had taken place we shouldn't have known it. We were not doing the sound effects, but there was a good deal of noise, Mr. Latimer and Mr. Hughes directing through megaphones, and so on, and we were all very excited. Mr. Latimer expects us all to feel our parts. He's not one of those directors who drive the extras like sheep. We are told what is happening. We've only just started on this picture, but we've done enough to see that it's going to be great, it's going to make film history."

Collier was very much impressed by the fervour with which they all spoke in praise of their young director. "It's going to be a thousand pities if we have to pull him in," he said to Duffield. "What a waste."

Sturt, who was deputising for the two directors, had been informed that the unit was free to go back to Town. No time was being lost, for as the two detectives came out of the bar where they had lunched hurriedly on beer and sandwiches, two motor-coaches drew up outside the hotel annex, and a crowd carrying suitcases trickled out of the revolving doors.

"Well, that clears the decks," said Duffield. "What next?"

"Back to Wells. Latimer is being taken care of. I think we can trust the secretary to look after him. The Arden girl will do very well under the motherly eye of Mrs. Trask. I'm glad we were able to get her back. We've spent half the day eliminating suspects. It's time we paid a little attention to young Condamine. The 'Constable' story is going to give us a useful lever."

"The tide is out," said Duffield, disappointed.

"Never mind, Sergeant. No time for a dip," said Collier, though he, too, looked wistfully across the shining sands at the wooded islands and the silver line of sea before he turned to the long row of parked cars. "Hallo, Grinstead. You got some lunch, I hope?"

"Yes, sir. Thank you, sir," lied Grinstead.

Collier nodded absently and got in the back of the car, leaving Duffield to sit by the driver. He was beginning to be aware of a very unpleasant sensation he had experienced more than once before while working on a case, and which is familiar to most people in nightmares, the feeling that there is something urgent to be done combined with a dreadful uncertainty as to what the thing may be. It did not help him that on previous occasions his anxiety had been justified. A hunch? Prevision? A manifestation of the subconscious? Whatever it was he was inclined to take it seriously.

He tapped on the glass when they had left the narrow main street of Axbridge behind them and said, "As fast as you can make it, please." Grinstead dutifully accelerated and immediately afterwards had to slow down to get past a herd of cows on their way to be milked. Collier gnawed his lower lip. "Steady—" he told himself.

They were getting on. The road followed the line of the Mendips, past the turning for Wookey and down into the green valley in which Wells lay drowsing in the mellow light of the autumn afternoon.

They stopped first at the hotel where they learned that Mr. Latimer and his friend had gone out in his car, taking a picnic lunch. Collier frowned. This was not what he had meant when he asked Hughes to look after their prime suspect, but he saw that if Latimer was determined to go out his secretary could hardly prevent him, and it was natural enough that he should not wish to remain shut up in his room.

They went on to the police station and met the police surgeon just coming out.

"The very man I wanted to see." He drew Collier aside.

"You want the post-mortem results. The fracture at the base of the skull was caused by two blows. The first, a glancing blow, knocked her down and she struck her forehead against that tree trunk in falling. The second finished the job as she lay. A nasty business, and I hope whoever did it swings for it. But there's something else which may or may not be relevant. She was four months gone in the family way."

"Irrelevant, I should imagine," said Collier slowly. "I shall have to think it over. I suppose her family knew. She would hardly make a secret of it. Wait a minute though. Wouldn't this affect the entail?"

"I doubt if anyone knew," said the doctor. "George would have told me. He wanted a child and was very disappointed that Ida had failed him so far. He would have been so delighted, poor fellow, so proud and pleased, he couldn't have kept it to himself. Besides, I'm the family doctor, not that I make much out of them. They're all aggressively healthy. But he'd have wanted to have me fussing over her. Perhaps that's why she kept it dark, because she hated fuss."

"A posthumous son for George Condamine would have been rather a let-down for his nephew," said Collier reflectively.

The doctor looked at him oddly. "How right you are. Well, I must be getting along. Some of my patients are still alive."

A stout constable in the charge-room was filling up forms. The scratching of his pen sounded loud in the quiet room where the only other sound was an occasional long-drawn whine from a stray dog shut up in the kennel in the yard awaiting his lawful owner. The constable stood up as the two men from the Yard came in.

"The Super had to go out, sir. I was to say that no further reports have come in and no phone calls."

"A blank, my lord," muttered Collier. Aloud he said, "Very well. When the Superintendent comes in tell him Grinstead is running us over to Baring. I must have a look round there."

"Yes, sir." The constable's large and rather unintelligent face brightened perceptibly. "Now I think of it, there was a message. If you should be seeing Miss Arden, sir, would you tell her Mrs. Trask rang up from Taunton to say her daughter's doing nicely now, and she'll be back along about nine o'clock."

Collier whirled round. "What did you say?"

The constable's jaw dropped. "Beg pardon, sir?"

"Didn't Mrs. Trask come back to the Manor last night? I understood that she was brought back from Taunton."

"Yes, sir. But she went back this morning to spend the day along with her daughter up to the hospital. I—I'm sorry if that's wrong, sir. 'Twas nothing to do with I—"

"No." Collier tried to be just. "A misunderstanding. Come along, Duffield—" He hurried out and his colleague followed. The constable, whose florid complexion had deepened to the hue of a ripe plum, stared after him in bewilderment. "Well, I'm—I don't know what this place is coming to—"

He heard a clash of gears that meant that Harry Grinstead, driving the police car, was being hustled, too. "London ways," he said, and went slowly back to his forms.

Chapter XV
A CONFESSION

Little Baring Manor turned a blind white face towards the empty shell of Great Baring which, at this hour, lay in shadow on the rising ground across the Valley. Blind. Deaf to knocking on the closed door, and silent when the echoes died away.

The two men from the Yard looked at one another, and Collier beckoned to the driver of their car to join them. Grinstead switched off the engine and came up the steps.

"Nobody at home?"

"She should be here. She promised," said Collier. "I don't like it. Knock again, Sergeant."

Duffield complied. They waited, but nothing happened. The lines in the Inspector's lean brown face seemed to have deepened. His colleague, looking at him, saw that some fear had taken shape in his mind. He said, "We can try the back door, and, if that is locked too, there's the larder window."

"Is it large enough?"

"I doubt if I could squeeze in, but this young chap here should be able to manage it."

Collier nodded. "Stay here, Sergeant Grinstead, you come with me." They went round the house by a dank path through an overgrown laurel shrubbery into the brick-paved stable yard. Stables and loose boxes had long been empty, and time had stopped, for the clock over the coach-house, at ten to twelve. The coach-house had been converted into a garage, but the Condamines' car which Ida Condamine had left just off the road when she went up through the woods to meet, as she hoped, a lover, had been towed up to Wells to be examined for finger-prints.

Collier tried the back door. It was locked and bolted. It opened, as he remembered, into a combined scullery and washhouse. The window over the sink and the larger kitchen window were screened by curtain of close white net so that it was useless to try to peer in.

"You'll have to get through the larder window and let us in, Grinstead. Yes, I know all about search warrants. But this may be urgent. I'm afraid it is."

"Yes, sir. Anything you say, sir."

Collier produced a clasp-knife fitted with various gadgets as they followed the path that led past the larder. "We've paid a good deal of attention to this window already. It is usually left open and the wire screen that is supposed to keep flies out is easily pushed aside, which means that possibly—but never mind that now—" He was already at work with the blade of his knife. The young constable looked on, grinning. "If you weren't on our side, sir, you might take up house-breaking."

"So I might." The window swung open. "Now then, in with you. Be careful. This shelf is clear. Mind the bread crock—"

The shelves were bare but for a few pots of jam, a jug half full of milk and an opened tin of baked beans.

Grinstead crawled in and closed the window again and Collier hurried round to the back door. The bolts were being drawn as he reached it. He stepped inside and looked about him. Draining-board and sink had been well scrubbed and were dry. Nothing seemed out of place. He went into the kitchen. The fire in the range was out and the ashes cold. The oil cooking stove was out. Here, too, everything was neat and clean, no dirty saucepans, no unwashed plate or crockery. Collier, after a quick glance round, went down the stone-paved passage through the baize-covered door into the hall. Already, though George

Condamine had not been dead a week, the bulb catalogues, the dog's lead, the old periodicals and odds and ends had been cleared away, and the place seemed unlived in. All the doors leading to the ground floor rooms were closed.

"Let the sergeant in, Grinstead. He must be tired of standing on the mat."

"Yes, sir."

Collier looked into the drawing-room. It smelt faintly musty and there was a thin film of dust over everything.

He went next to the little room called the study on the left of the front door where he had interviewed Ida Condamine. It looked exactly as it had done then. An exclamation from Duffield recalled him. The stout sergeant was standing on the threshold of a room at the back of the hall.

"She's here—"

Collier remembered the room. Lucy Arden had told him that they used it both for meals and for sitting in, and that when George and his brother were boys it had been their playroom and glory hole. "It's the warmest room in the house and the most cheerful," she had said. It was comfortably furnished with a big divan and armchairs in loose covers of faded chintz. The carpet was threadbare, but so were all the others. There was a bookcase filled with shabby and well-thumbed novels ranging from the yellow-backed railway novels of the 'nineties to the latest Penguins.

Lucy had always liked this room and she was here now, lying on the big divan, looking not much bigger than a child in her black and white frock. She seemed to be asleep. A cup and saucer stood on the floor within reach of the hand that hung down. There were dregs of coffee in the cup.

Collier bent over her, listening to her difficult, stertorous breathing. He felt her pulse. His face was very grave.

"Drugged?" said Duffield.

"It seems so. Probably one of the barbiturates. Take care of that cup."

"There's a letter on the table addressed to the coroner."

"Leave it for the moment. We may be in time—"

"Shall I take the car and fetch the doctor and a nurse, sir?" suggested Grinstead.

"No. It will be quicker to take her directly to the hospital. Get a couple of blankets from one of the beds upstairs. You'll drive and the sergeant will sit with her at the back. The sooner the better."

The blankets were fetched and wrapped round the small inert body and Grinstead ran out to start the engine while the other two carried her out between them.

"Get her there as fast as you can. They'll know what to do at the hospital. Tell them nobody is to be allowed near her for any reason whatsoever. Then come back here."

Collier turned and went back into the house as the car started.

Grinstead drove fast down the avenue and slowed down and sounded his horn before he turned into the main road.

"Looks like you've got what you were looking for," he said. "I suppose she was always one of the suspects."

Duffield was steadying the muffled figure at his side with a ham-like but not ungentle hand. "We couldn't help seeing she had the opportunity and what some might call a motive," he said cautiously. "Keep going as fast as you can without risking an accident. Her breathing isn't as good as it was."

"It might be best for her if it stopped," said the younger man.

"That's not for us to say. It's our duty to keep her alive."

At the hospital not a minute was wasted. Lucy was lifted on to a stretcher and carried in. Duffield followed, and came back to the car after a few words with the house surgeon and the matron.

"O.K.," he said as he got in beside the driver. "Back to the Manor. Step on it."

"Will she live?"

"They don't know."

Neither spoke again until Grinstead drew up at the foot of the Manor house steps. Then the sergeant said, "Wait in the car. I'll call you if you're wanted."

The door was on the latch. He crossed the silent, empty hall to the room where they had found the girl and, as he did so, he glanced at his wrist-watch. They had been gone thirty-five minutes.

Collier was seated at the table with the letter and the envelope that had contained it spread out before him, studying them thoughtfully as he might have read a map. "There you are. What did they say?"

"Nothing much. Not very hopeful, I fancy. But I was to tell you we were right to bring her along. They've got all the doings there. They'll save her if it's humanly possible."

Collier sighed. "Listen to this."

Duffield came over to stand beside him and looked over his shoulder at the pencilled scrawl. "A confession?"

"Cousin Julia came to see me this morning. She said I could stay until I found somewhere to go and that she was sorry if she had seemed hard. She was really very kind, but she looked at me queerly and I think she suspects though she can't actually know. I'm so tired, I feel I can't go on, and there's really nothing much to live for now. The five hundred pounds George left me would not last very long. I'm just going to take some of Ida's sleeping stuff and end it. You may as well know the truth and stop the police from bothering people who had nothing whatever to do with it. I killed George, though I didn't mean to. The sandwiches were for her. I never thought he might eat them. I've always hated her. If only he hadn't gone to Bournemouth that time and met her he would have married me. If she had been a good wife to him I might have forgiven her, but she wasn't. She had lovers, more than one, I'm sure. I stayed on working like a servant, counting for nothing in the house where I might have been the mistress. You can't blame me for feeling bitter. About what happened yesterday—no, the day before. I get muddled about times. The assistant director said I might come and see them taking scenes at the pool. I told Cousin Julia about it and she said she would come too. I soon got tired of it, and I left her there and started to walk home through the woods. I hadn't gone far when I saw Ida hurrying up the path that leads to the ruined cottage. She didn't see me. I wondered what she was up to so I followed at a safe distance. She never looked round. She crossed the clearing, forcing her way through the bracken, and sat down on a heap of rubble just inside the cottage, and looked at her watch and lit a cigarette. I guessed she was waiting for that film director. I knew she was in love with him. She was sitting with her back to me. I picked up a lump of rock and crept up behind her. I need not tell you what I did nor why. She was a wicked, selfish, grasping, immoral woman. She had nothing but her beauty, and her beauty was a curse. I thought Mr. Latimer would be suspected. I didn't care. It served him right for getting mixed up with her. Men are such fools. But I may as well tell you the whole truth now that I've finished with everything.

"LUCY ARDEN."

"Gosh," said Duffield. "So that's how it was."

"Perhaps," said Collier.

"Why? Don't you believe her? It sounds like the truth to me."

"In part. But I don't think it's the whole truth. Let's reconstruct this attempted suicide. I've been through it once and I'll go through it again with you. Mrs. Luke Condamine called this morning, presumably after the housekeeper had left for Taunton. We shall be able to get corroborative evidence from her there. After she left, the girl decided to put an end to herself. She fetched down a bottle of sleeping tablets from Ida Condamine's room. I found the bottle here on the floor hidden by the frill of the divan's loose cover. It's there on the table. Don't touch it. As you see, there are only two tablets left. Then she went to the kitchen and made herself some coffee. After making it she let it grow tepid while she washed the coffee jug and the milk saucepan and put them away. Then she came here, took an overdose of tablets, washed them down with coffee and lay down on the divan. Previously, of course, she had written this confession addressed to the coroner, presumably with the pencil which I found where it had rolled under the table."

Duffield looked at him warily. "Well, what's wrong with that?"

"Nothing, perhaps. But why coffee? A glass of water or a drink of milk would have been less trouble. Perhaps she was very fond of coffee and thought she would give herself a final treat. But, in that case, would she have let it get cold while she washed the jug and the saucepan?"

"She might," argued Duffield. "She would be flurried, all of a dither. I remember my old mother, if she was upset, picking up a thing and putting it down again and not knowing what to do next."

"Very well. Though the confession shows no trace of that sort of mental confusion. There is one other thing."

"What is it?"

"I dusted the bottle of tablets for finger-prints."

"Well?"

"There aren't any."

This kind of concrete evidence was more likely to impress the sergeant than any theories about Lucy Arden's state of mind. He eyed the film of yellow powder on the little bottle reflectively. "They might have got rubbed off on the carpet. What's in your mind, Inspector?"

"Nothing definite. This may be the end of our case. But I want it proved up to the hilt. A confession is not enough. You know that, Duffield. There have been plenty of bogus confessions in our experience. People dramatize themselves. In this case it may be a form of wish fulfilment. I don't doubt that the girl hated Ida Condamine. She'd had a raw deal here. A good deal of what I've just read to you rang true enough. And yet, somehow, it's phoney." He frowned at the sheet of notepaper lying on the table and turned it over gingerly. "I'm going up now to the place where the murder was committed. I want to go over it thoroughly before the light fails. We can't keep those fellows on guard at the gates indefinitely. I want you to do something here first."

He gave some further instructions. Duffield nodded. "If there is any, I'll find it. If not—"

"If not, it will be the murderer's mistake. Come after us to the ruined cottage."

Grinstead had given the car a polish while he waited and got back into the driving-seat. He was getting bored and impatient, but he brightened up, and when Collier called him he came eagerly.

"Yes, sir?"

"We're going through Little Baring woods to the clearing where the body was found, and, as I'm in a hurry, we're going more or less as the crow flies."

"There's always been a path, sir, from the Manor, though it may be overgrown. I've heard tell of it. They called it Witch Way. The tale is that one of the Condamines a long time since was sweet on a girl that lived up at the cottage in the wood and the path was made by them meeting half-way. It's the story they've got hold of for a film."

They were crossing the park. A constable in uniform was standing by the gate in the palings.

"Anything to report?"

"No, sir. I saw the lady that lives down the road, Mrs. Luke Condamine, go up to the Manor this morning and go back after a bit. She came up to ask if I'd had any breakfast, and said she was glad it wasn't raining as I had to be here. A very pleasant-spoken lady."

"Anyone else?"

"Not to my knowledge, sir. But I can't see the avenue nor the house from here, and it's too far off to say if motor traffic is along the road or coming up to the Manor."

Collier nodded. "Your relief will be here soon."

The wood was dense, with a good deal of undergrowth. It would be easy to follow a trail and remain unseen. It was probably here, where two paths intersected, that the killer had first caught sight of the quarry and turned aside. *I picked up a lump of rock. I need not tell you what I did or why.* The jury who heard that read out in court would not hesitate long over their verdict. Whatever the previous provocation, it was an ugly, cold-blooded business. Why was he so reluctant to take her word for it? More evidence. What did he hope to find in that lonely clearing where the crumbling walls and gaunt skeleton rafters of the witch's hovel lay half buried in bracken and briars? *I picked up a lump of rock.* They had found the rock smeared with blood and with long black hairs adhering to it. He stopped short. She must be guilty. How else could she have known what had been done? No particulars had been given to the Press, only a vague reference to severe head injuries.

He looked at his companion who stood waiting patiently for him to go on. "Have you that parcel I gave you to carry?"

"Yes, sir."

"Two shoes. Mrs. Condamine wore size three and went in for high heels. Miss Arden's is a five, a stout country shoe. I want you to look out for footprints. There's very little open ground, unfortunately. Too much bracken."

Grinstead had sharp eyes. He found a footprint in the moist earth where a spring had made the ground swampy only a few yards from the spot where the path entered the clearing. Ida Condamine's smart red kid slipper fitted it exactly.

"Good. See if you can find any others. Not much hope really. Most of the ground was trampled over by the police yesterday when she was found. But you may be lucky."

He left Grinstead to his search, and forced his way through the tall yellow bracken until he stood where he had been standing twenty-four hours earlier, looking down at where she lay, all passion spent.

Was it true that the earth-bound dead came back to re-enact their tragedies? Had the gipsy who had been hunted to her death three hundred years ago lived again in Ida Condamine? Such fancies were not for him, and he dismissed them from his mind. There, half hidden in a tangled growth of rosebay willow herb, was the blackened hearth stone on which a fire had burned and forbidden potions simmered, fat from a gibbet, the heart of a toad.

Something glittered in the coarse grass just by his foot. He stooped to pick it up and looked at it as it lay in his palm. And as he turned it over, the pieces of the puzzle fell into place.

CHAPTER XVI

THE BROKEN STRING

OSWALD Condamine was spending an evening at home. He lay on the sofa, smoking cigarettes and turning the pages of a novel. The October evenings were chilly and his mother had lit the fire and was sitting close to it and warming her thin hands at the blaze.

"I might be able to sell the Manor for a road house if only we were nearer Bath or Bristol," he said. "As it is, the blasted place is a white elephant."

"We shall have to live there for a time at any rate, Ozzie."

"I suppose so. With electric light and a telephone it will be just habitable," he conceded. "I'll have that put in hand at once."

She looked at him doubtfully. "It will cost a good deal. George got an estimate soon after he married. Ida wanted it. But he didn't feel he could afford it."

"George was an old stick-in-the-mud. I can get an advance from old Rand."

"Of course. You have to pay off that horrid man at Weston."

He frowned. "Never mind about that," he said roughly. "I'm sorry now I told you about it. I shouldn't have done if I hadn't thought you might be able to help me out. Savings."

"I used to have. But I've had to help you before now."

"That's right," he grumbled, "nag, nag. Don't let me forget it."

"Oh, Ozzie, don't be unkind when I'm so worried."

He turned his head and looked at her with more attention than he often bestowed on her. "What's the matter with you? What are you worrying about? I don't care for the police prying into my affairs any more than you do, but it won't last much longer, and actually we're sitting pretty. Think of that picture and what I shall get for it, so cheer up."

She bent forward to poke the fire, and the bangles jingled on her bony wrists. "If only the man they send to value the furniture for probate doesn't realize its value."

"Would it matter if he did?"

"Of course. It would make an immense difference to the death duties."

"Oh. I see."

"He's not likely to be a judge of pictures," she said, trying to reassure herself. "It isn't noticeable hanging in that dark corner, and it's very dirty. The dining-room chimney has smoked when the wind was in the south-west ever since I can remember. You've never spoken of what I told you about it to another soul, have you, Ozzie?"

"What do you take me for?" he said, wondering if she would guess that he had boasted of the "Constable" to Caston when he was persuading him to wait for repayment of the money he had—well—borrowed, and spent on the dogs and taking out that brassy-haired little slut in Caston's office. But Caston would keep his mouth shut. Or would he?

"We shall have to wait until the will is proved and everything settled before we discover it," she said. "You must see that, Ozzie. We can't have people saying that we knew about it and didn't tell George. It wouldn't look well."

"Keeping up appearances," he jeered, but he added, though ungraciously, "I expect you're right."

She had picked up her knitting and put it down again. "I wonder what they're doing. Do you think that Inspector is clever?"

"How should I know? I don't think about it. Let the police get on with the job. It's their worry, not ours. Anyhow, it's fairly obvious who bumped Ida off."

"Is it?"

"Latimer, of course. You must have noticed the way she looked at him and he didn't look at her that afternoon at the Manor. Nothing more apt to make a chap feel murderous than to be chased by a skirt when he's browned off, sick of the sight of her."

"I shall be glad when it's over," she said. "It's very unsettling. I think I'll go to bed now."

"All right. I'll just finish this chapter."

She stopped on her way out to kiss him. "Good night, my darling."

He answered absently, his eyes on his book. "Good night, old thing. Sleep well."

The sofa springs creaked under his weight as he settled himself more comfortably to follow the hair-raising escapes of a private dick who, on a diet of hamburgers and alcohol, made love to every woman he met while he bluffed his way through the jungle of American Big Business. After a while he began to yawn. He was thinking of following his mother upstairs when the bell rang. He got off the sofa, grumbling, and went to the door. Peering into the darkness he made out three shadowy figures.

"What is it? What do you want?"

A west-country voice answered. "You know me, Mr. Condamine, Superintendent Bostock from Wells. I'm with Detective-Inspector Collier and Detective-Sergeant Duffield. We'd like a few words with you, please."

"You've chosen a funny time. Oh, all right. Come in."

They followed him into the lamplit sitting-room.

"Park yourselves," said the fat youth hospitably. "What about drinks? No whisky left, but there's some cider. Cigarettes?"

"No, thank you, sir. Is Mrs. Condamine at home?"

"She's gone to bed. It's past eleven, you know."

"We are later than we meant to be," said Collier. "There were calls to be put through and so forth. Now, Mr. Condamine, it is my duty to tell you that you need not answer questions, and that if you do anything you say may be used later on in evidence."

Ozzie paused in the act of striking a match to stare at him.

"I say! That sounds ominous. What's the big idea?"

"You have always been out when we called. This is the first opportunity I have had to check up on your alibi for the day before yesterday. Where were you during that afternoon and evening?"

Ozzie seemed relieved. "Is that all? I went over to Weston on my motor-cycle in the morning and got there about eleven. It was early closing and I had arranged to meet a girl who works in a draper's shop. We had lunch and went to a movie. I forget the name of the main feature, but Betty Hutton was starring in it. After that we went on to a roadhouse and mucked about there until she said I must take her home or she'd get into trouble with her auntie. I got back here soon after one and went straight to bed."

"Good. What cinema was it?"

Ozzie gave the name readily.

"And the roadhouse?"

"The Blue Crocodile. On the Bristol road."

"And the name of the young lady?"

"Can't you leave the kid alone? It won't do her any good if the police come barging around."

"We won't do that, Mr. Condamine. I'm afraid we must have it."

Ozzie grinned. "Very well. Her name is Bibs. I don't know her surname. Anything else?"

"Will you ask your mother to come down?"

"I told you she's gone to bed. You'd better come again in the morning."

"I'm sorry, Mr. Condamine. The matter is urgent She was with Miss Arden on Wednesday afternoon watching the film unit taking some scenes. I must tell you that Miss Arden to-day took an overdose of a narcotic, and that a written confession addressed to the coroner was found. Mrs. Condamine, having seen her so recently, may be able to help us."

Ozzie gazed at him open-mouthed. "Lucy. You don't mean to say it was Lucy? Well, I'm damned. I didn't think she had it in her. Lucy. I thought—all right, I'll fetch my mother."

When he had gone out, Duffield got up and went over to the bureau. He was back in his place and thoughtfully nibbling the end of his pencil when the young man returned. Julia Condamine was with him.

"This is frightful," she said, "simply frightful. I can't believe it. Of course I've always known poor Lucy brooded over what I suppose she thought of as her wrongs. But even so it's—it's horrifying. Three deaths in less than a week—"

The Superintendent opened his mouth to speak, caught Collier's eye and thought better of it.

"It is my duty to warn you," said Collier. "You may assist the police by making a statement, but anything you say now will be taken down and may be used in evidence."

"Of course." She glanced at Duffield, who had opened his notebook and was writing busily. Her eyes and teeth glittered in the lamplight as she leaned forward in her chair with her habitual air of restless eager interest "Anything I can do—"

"Will you tell us all you can remember about Wednesday afternoon?"

"I was going down to the church to see if the flowers in the altar vases needed changing, but I met Lucy and she told me the assistant director, you know—that little Welshman, Davies, is it, or Evans—"

"Hughes," said Collier.

"Oh, is it? Anyway, he had told her she might watch the film people at work if she was very quiet and kept well behind the cameras. I thought it might be rather fun, so I went with her. Mr. What-is-it placed a couple of deckchairs for us where we shouldn't be in the way, but he couldn't stay with us as he had to dance attendance on the great Mr. Latimer. It was quite interesting. Groups of people, all in the seventeenth-century costumes, were being taken as they jostled one another on the marshy ground at the edge of the pool. The two directors were shouting orders through megaphones and rushing about telling people to put a sock in it. But it went on and on and I began to feel chilly. Lucy said she thought she would go home. I stayed a few minutes longer. I went back by the short cut across the park, and I didn't go out again."

"Can you recall anything of your conversation with Miss Arden?"

"Nothing of any importance. Lucy never has had much to say for herself. I asked her how Ida was, and she said she had gone out in her car that morning and had not returned. We hardly spoke while we were watching the film people since we had been warned to be quiet."

"How were your chairs placed?"

"On the rising ground with the wood just at the back of us. The gate through which we had come and by which we left the field was just on our right."

"Were you quite alone there?"

"There was a row of chairs in front of us, but they were unoccupied. As we arrived, I saw Mr. Latimer sitting in one of them, but he jumped up and went to speak to the camera men and he did not come back."

"He left his coat, didn't he, hanging on the back of his chair?"

"Did he? He may have done. I didn't notice."

"You did not take a letter from his coat pocket, read it, and replace it?"

"Certainly not."

"Before you went home did you go up the hill through the wood to the ruined cottage in the clearing?"

"I did not."

Collier looked at her thoughtfully. A dark red flush had come out in patches on her sallow face and thin neck. The prominent eyes looked strained. She turned to the local Superintendent and said loudly, "This man is being insulting. I demand protection."

The Superintendent appeared uncomfortable. He mumbled, "I am sorry, madam. Very sorry—"

Ozzie, who had been gazing at his mother with growing dismay, tried to restrain her. "Steady on, Mater."

Collier took a small tin box from his overcoat pocket, opened it and held it out for inspection.

"Crystal and jet beads. You were wearing a string of such beads the other day, Mrs. Condamine. Could you identify them as yours?"

She made an evident and painful effort to regain self-control, compressing her lips and twisting her thin hands together.

"They—look like mine."

"The string broke and they were scattered. How was that, and where did it happen?"

"I have no idea. I gave the string to Lucy. She took a great fancy to it."

"When was this?"

"The other afternoon."

"While you were watching the taking of the picture?"

"Yes."

"I see," said Collier. "Mrs. Condamine, you must come with us. We have a policewoman waiting outside. She will go upstairs with you while you get together what you require for the night. You will come before the magistrates to-morrow morning."

She licked her dry lips. "What for? What am I charged with?"

"We have a warrant with us. You are charged with the murder of your sister-in-law, Ida Condamine."

"You fool," she said shrilly, "you'll be turned out of the Force for this. You've got Lucy's confession. You're mad. You're all mad—"

Ozzie Condamine sat down heavily and covered his face with his hands. When he looked up there was no one in the room but Collier and there was blood running down his jaw from a deep scratch and his tie was hanging loose under one ear.

"Oh God," stammered Ozzie, his fat face quivering. "She isn't—you didn't hurt her—"

"No." The Inspector's voice was unexpectedly kind. "It's a bad show for you. Get in touch with your lawyer the first thing to-morrow. To-night would be even better. You could ring him up from Wells. She should have someone to represent her at the police court. The inquest doesn't matter so much. It will be adjourned almost at once. Have a drink and pull yourself together. She will be depending on you."

"Thanks. You—you're being very decent," quavered poor Ozzie.

The inquest on Ida Condamine was opened the following morning at ten o'clock and adjourned indefinitely after evidence of identification had been given by the family lawyer, Mr. Rand.

At eleven Julia Condamine was brought before the magistrates, a full Bench, sitting in the police court. She was represented by Mr. Rand, who looked pale and perturbed; and pleaded not guilty and reserved her defence. The barrister briefed for the Crown asked for a remand to give him time to prepare his case and was granted two days. At the second hearing he made a short but telling speech.

"The body of the murdered woman was found at a certain spot in the woods which are a part of the Condamine estate. Subsequently fragments of a letter were found which she had written to a friend asking him to meet her there. Suspicion naturally fell upon this gentleman. In the statement he made to the police he admitted receiving the letter but said he had no intention of meeting Mrs. Condamine, and that, in fact, he drove to Taunton and spent the evening there. The officers in charge of the case, after interviewing a number of witnesses, went over to Condamine Manor to interview Miss Arden, a member of the household. They found her in one of the rooms downstairs, lying on a sofa in an unconscious condition. She had evidently taken an overdose of some soporific drug. She was removed to the hospital and a thorough search was made of the premises. The officer in charge, Detective-Inspector Collier, made a note of some points that struck him as strange, so that, in spite of a written confession, signed 'Lucy Arden', and addressed to the coroner, he kept an open mind. He next returned to the scene of the crime. He had posted constables to prevent anyone from entering the wood by either of the two gates after the discovery of the body. On this second visit to the spot he found a number of black and crystal beads lying in the long grass. He had previously seen Mrs. Luke Condamine, the accused, wearing a string of similar beads. Pursuing his investigation in the light of this discovery, he interviewed the director and the assistant director of the film company that has been making a picture on the late Mr. Condamine's land. I only propose to call three witnesses. I think their evidence will suffice to show that there is a case to go to the Assizes. I call Stephen Latimer."

Latimer, who looked drawn and haggard, but was more carefully dressed than usual, and evidently, to those who knew him, on his best behaviour, repeated the solemn words of the oath, not in a meaningless legal gabble but as if he meant them. The beautiful voice rang through the court, and the public at the back of the court prepared to be thrilled.

"On Wednesday afternoon, you were directing the taking of some scenes for a film?"

"Yes."

"You received a note reminding you that the writer expected you to meet her at a place already agreed upon?"

"Yes. It was given to me by one of the extras. It had been handed to him by a boy in the lane. I read it and tore it up and thought no more about it. I was very much occupied at the time."

"Did you intend to keep the appointment?"

"No. I should explain that Mrs. Condamine was extremely anxious to take a part in the picture we are filming now. It was becoming quite an obsession with her. I had told her I did not think her husband would approve. I was afraid she meant to reopen the subject."

"The fragments of the letter you tore up were collected and put together. Is this it?"

"Yes. To the best of my recollection. I read it hurriedly."

"It was a reminder. She had written previously?"

"Yes. I had a letter from her by that morning's post"

"Had you destroyed that?"

"No. It was in the pocket of my coat."

"You were in your shirt-sleeves while you were directing the crowd scenes before you changed into the clothes you wore while acting your part?"

"Yes. I took my coat off and hung it over the back of my chair. It was brought to me when we had finished for the day and were packing up."

"Is this the letter? Don't touch it, please."

"Yes."

"Mrs. Luke Condamine and Miss Arden were sitting just behind the chair you had occupied during a part of the afternoon, were they not?"

"Yes. I saw them and was rather annoyed. Hughes had invited them. He should have known better. I don't have people looking on when I am working."

The chairman of the Bench spoke. "Is all this relevant, Mr. Spencer?"

"I think so, your worship. Our case is that the accused saw the letter. It may have fallen out of the witness's coat pocket as it hung over the back of his chair. We say that she read it and put it back, having learned that her sister-in-law would be waiting at a certain spot at a certain hour, and that she foresaw that if she was attacked suspicion might fall on Mr. Latimer."

"Is this all supposition?"

"No, your worship. This letter has been tested for finger-prints. It has been handled by three people; by the writer, who has since been done to death; by the witness who received it; and by the accused."

There was a perceptible movement in the crowded courtroom which was instantly stilled as the examination of the witness was resumed.

"Had you met Ida Condamine previously at the place where her body was found? In the letter she says at the witch's cottage, which should be mine."

"I can explain that. I came down three weeks ago and stayed at the Manor. I had been invited by Mr. Condamine, who was very keen for me to make a picture founded on a family legend. My assistant and secretary came with me. We were to hear the story and be shown the traditional sites which might be used as a background. On the afternoon after our arrival, Mrs. Condamine took me for a walk through the woods to the ruins of the cottage which figures in the tragedy. The part she wished to play was that of a gipsy girl who, with her mother, was accused of witchcraft, hunted down by the villagers and drowned in Baring Pool. We talked it over there. She was very persuasive and almost convinced me, but not quite—"

"Yes, yes. That is quite clear. There were no other meetings?"

"Certainly not. I agreed with Mr. Condamine that we would make the picture and went back to London the next day to get on with the job. I never saw either Mr. or Mrs. Condamine again."

"Thank you. That will be all for the present, Mr. Latimer."

Latimer went to his seat at the back of the court. He looked calm enough, and no one was to know that the palms of his hands were wet.

The next witness was Sergeant Duffield. His stolid unemotional narrative made its own impression. He described how he and the Inspector in charge of the investigation had forced an entry to the Manor and found Lucy Arden in a drugged stupor on the sofa in one of the ground floor rooms, with a coffee cup containing dregs of coffee on the floor beside her, and a bottle of sleeping tablets, with two tablets remaining in it, partly hidden by the frill of the loose cover. There was an envelope on the table addressed to the coroner, and a pencil was subsequently found under the table.

"It was an end of a lead pencil?"

"Yes."

"There was in the envelope a sheet of paper with what purported to be a confession, signed 'Lucy Arden'?"

"Yes."

"It was written in pencil?"

"Yes."

"With the pencil you found?"

"No"

"Why not?"

"The pencil on the floor was an H.B. The confession was written with a B."

"Did you find any writing-paper in the house «mi1ar to that used for the confession?"

"No. I found two writing-paper blocks, partly used, one in Mr. Condamine's bureau and the other with a packet of envelopes, in Miss Arden's suitcase, which was partly packed, and was under the bed in her room. These blocks were similar in size and of the quality and make of some that are now on sale in a chain store in the High Street. The paper on which the confession was written is of a rather better quality."

"Did you subsequently find a block of identical paper?"

"Yes."

"Was it in a desk in the living-room of Mrs. Luke Condamine's cottage?"

"It was."

"After Miss Arden had been removed to the hospital, did you proceed to the spot in the woods where the murder had been committed?"

"Yes. The Inspector was there before me. He showed me some jet and crystal beads he had picked up near where the body had lain."

"Had you seen the accused wearing these or similar beads?"

"Yes."

"Thank you, Sergeant. That will be all."

The chairman consulted with his fellow magistrates before he turned again to the barrister appearing for the Crown.

"Have you any more witnesses?"

"There are a considerable number whom we could call, your worship, but actually we thought it might suffice to produce one more at this time. She has come forward voluntarily to give evidence which serves to indicate a motive for this crime."

"Does that mean that Miss Arden is sufficiently recovered to give her version of the affair?"

"Unfortunately, no, your worship. I understand that Miss Arden is still on the danger list."

"Very well."

Mr. Spencer looked towards the door by which the witnesses entered the court room. "Call Bessie Cullen." Bessie Cullen was a tall woman neatly dressed in black. She had evidently been a handsome girl and her weather-beaten face still showed some traces of her lost beauty. She repeated the words of the oath clearly in her soft, west-country drawl and stood resting her work-worn hands on the wooden rail before her and waiting placidly to be questioned.

"You are a widow, Mrs. Cullen?"

"Yes, sir."

"You earn a livelihood by going out scrubbing, and sometimes you hawk fish?"

"Yes."

"You had some fish to sell last Tuesday?"

"Yes. Me and my grandson were out with the donkey and cart, and we didn't do so bad. A bit of fish is a change like to the folks living up along."

"Did you call at the cottage of Mrs. Luke Condamine?"

"I did. I told the boy to take Neddy on to the village and I'd catch up with he. I got a sister there and I reckoned she'd give I a cup of tea. I went up to the door with my basket of fish, but I didn't ring the bell."

"Why not?"

"They was hollering away inside and the window was open so I could hear what they was saying. It was the two Mrs. Condamines, Mrs. Luke and her from the Manor what Mr. George married. She'd got one of they London voices. You couldn't mistake it. Anyways, Mrs. Luke called her by her name. 'You're lying, Ida,' she says, 'trying to do my poor Ozzie out of what is his by right.' And Mrs. George, she laughed in an aggravating sort of way, and 'Wait and see,' her says. 'I'm going to a doctor in Bath to-morrow, and if he confirms it, as he will, I shall tell Mr. Rand. I'm sorry to disappoint you, Julia darling, but George's son will inherit. If you behave yourself I may allow you to live on here rent free, but don't count on it,' she says. Mrs. Luke made a queer sort of noise and called her a name I won't soil my lips with repeating, and the other, she laughed again. It reminded me of a neighbour I once had, a bad woman she was and she laughed like that once when she broke my little cat's back with a poker. I had her up for it, too, and her was fined five shillings. And I was frightened and thought I'd best be going, so I didn't hear no more."

"Thank you, Mrs. Cullen. That will be all."

"Thank you, sir," said Mrs. Cullen and bobbed a curtsey to the Bench before she left the box.

The chairman of the magistrates cleared his throat. "I understand that this evidence suggests that the deceased informed the accused that she was expecting a child?"

"That is the suggestion, your worship."

"Is it confirmed by the results of the post-mortem?"

"It is."

There was another whispered consultation on the Bench.

The result of it was that Julia Condamine was committed for trial at the next Assizes. She had sat quietly in the dock throughout, apparently taking no interest in the proceedings, and she stood up obediently as one of her attendant wardresses touched her arm, and went out with them to the car that was waiting. She even seemed unaware of the angry crowd trying to break through the strong police cordon as she was being driven away.

CHAPTER XVII
THE THIRD PICTURE

IT WAS some months later that Inspector Collier, buying an evening paper at the book stall in Victoria Station, was jostled by a man who turned to beg his pardon. The anxious monkey face and the musical Welsh voice were both familiar.

"Mr. Hughes?"

"Why, if it isn't the Inspector, look you." The dark eyes lit up. Evan Hughes seemed genuinely pleased to see him. "Come and have a drink?"

"No, thanks. Not just now. But I wouldn't mind a cup of tea."

Five minutes later they were seated at a marble-topped table garnished with the crumbs of a previous meal.

"She'll come when she's ready," said Collier, having failed to catch the eye of the waitress. "You're looking well, Mr. Hughes."

Evan grinned. "I've gained nearly a stone. Regular meals and all that. Lucy's a domestic tyrant."

"You married Miss Arden? Congratulations. And how's Mr. Latimer?"

Evan's expressive face clouded over. "Poor old Stephen. He should be here. *Black Magic* is having its world première at the Colonna in Leicester Square to-morrow. But he's gone to Hollywood. He had a good offer, and our people wouldn't stand in his way, though he's a great loss to us. *Black Magic* is his third picture and his best. It's had a rough passage. I suppose you know it was held up for weeks. It was a bit of luck for us that Julia Condamine didn't live to stand in the dock. If Latimer had got the wrong kind of publicity during the trial the studio executive meant to scrap the film. He realized that was inevitable. He made a fool of himself getting mixed up with that woman during those weeks in the summer when I wasn't there to look after him. It's on his mind that he was the indirect cause of poor George Condamine's death."

"I'm afraid that is so," said Collier. "We think she poisoned her husband, but we should not have been able to prove it. It certainly was fortunate for Latimer that there was no trial."

"What did she die of?"

"Cancer, deep-seated and unoperable. They couldn't do anything but keep her under morphia. Young Condamine's gone to Australia. So that's the end of the Condamines of Great and Little Baring. The property is in the market. It won't fetch much; but it seems there's a picture by Constable which is being sold at Christie's and which will probably fetch a large sum. I heard young Oswald hopes to buy a partnership in a bookmaking firm in Melbourne."

"Do you think he had anything to do with the murders?"

"No. He's a young twerp, selfish, self-indulgent, dishonest, but he's not a killer."

"There is one thing that was mentioned during the inquest that has always puzzled me," said Evan. "George Condamine called at the Rectory on his way home from that ill-fated picnic. The rector was out and he waited some time. The housekeeper's evidence indicated that he was suffering from shock. From the little I saw of him he was normally a very placid person."

"I remember. We could only guess at the cause, and guesses aren't evidence. I think myself that Ida had turned on him and said something that opened his eyes to what had been going on. The outing had been her suggestion, and perhaps the poor fellow had taken it as a sign of some softening in her attitude towards him and had tried to be affectionate. Something like that. No doubt her nerves were on edge. She may have been made reckless by the fact that the *al fresco* meal had been eaten and the poison was at work. Don't let your friend idealize his memories of her, Mr. Hughes. Her beauty was only skin deep. The essential Ida was as ugly as sin."

"I suppose so," said Evan sadly. "She was trying to put the blame on Lucy, wasn't she?"

"Yes. She was to be the scapegoat for Ida, and later for Julia Condamine. Her death was essential from the moment that Julia realized that her string of beads had been broken at the time of her attack on Ida. She couldn't get back into the woods to search for them as she would have done if I had not posted a cordon of police to watch out for that very thing. She could say she had given the beads to Miss Arden, but only if she was unable to contradict her. So Miss Arden must be silenced, and, at the same time, a faked confession would put an end to police enquiries. Or so she thought. She made several mistakes."

"Lucy says she came up to the house that morning and was kinder than usual, and told her she could stay on until she found somewhere to go. Then she said she would like coffee and would make some while Lucy looked for a book which she said she had lent to George and wanted to take home with her. Lucy said the coffee was unusually strong and very sweet and she only drank it because she was afraid of giving offence. She doesn't remember any more."

"I know," said Collier. He had read Lucy's statement. "The killer was in too great a hurry. She wrote the confession at home and left the block of paper and the pencil behind. Clumsy, very clumsy. De Quincy was right. Murder, if it is to be successful, is a fine art."

Evan looked at his watch. "I must be getting along. About the picture. Would you care to see it, Inspector? I could give you passes for a couple of seats for tomorrow."

Collier looked pleased. "That's very kind of you. I think I could get the evening off, and my wife would be thrilled."

"Good." Evan scribbled a few words on a card and passed it over. "Lucy won't be there. She hasn't been down to the Studios while it was being filmed. I don't want her to see it. A lot of the scenes would be familiar to her and would revive painful memories. It's an A film, you know. Rosamund Harper put up a terrific performance, really spine-chilling at moments. Stella was Latimer's leading lady, but Rosamund has stolen the picture, though Stella's pretty good, too. However often I see it I get a creepy feeling now and again. Don't bring Mrs. Collier if she's nervous."

"That's no way to stop her." They left the refreshment room together.

"Good Lord," said Evan. "I've just remembered. We never had any tea after all."

Collier looked after him smiling, as he hurried away. He looked definitely stronger, less harassed and unkempt. Lucy was equal to her job.

Sandra Collier was delighted, as her husband had known she would be, at the prospect of a break in the daily routine of housework and standing in shopping queues. They arrived at the Colonna in good time. The profits of the first performance were to be given to a charity, and a minor royalty and several celebrities of the stage and screen were to be present. The theatre was already crowded when the Colliers reached their seats in the dress circle. Sandra leaned forward eagerly as the lights went down. The title of the picture was shown against the ruined shell of Great Baring, dark against a stormy sky. The names of the technicians and the cast followed. Written and directed by Stephen Latimer. Assistant Director, Evan Hughes.

The story opened gaily with the three children playing in the hay-field while the little gipsy girl watched them through a gap in the hedge. Ten years passed and the four were seen again, the spoiled heiress from the great house losing her heart to the country boy, and learning, later, of his secret meetings with the gipsy whose mother was a reputed witch. From that point the action quickened through the coming to Wells of Matthew Hopkins and his two sinister assistants, the interviews at the inn, which were played exactly as Latimer and Evan had planned them, and the mounting suspense and excitement of the witch hunt, culminating in the scene at the pool.

Sandra clutched her husband's arm as Hugh Condamine lifted the girl's body on to his saddle. "Is she drowned? Is she dead? How awful—"

"Steady on, my dear. It's only a picture," he whispered. He was thinking that while this scene was being shot a murder was being committed. Vashti and Ida Condamine had died together, the sham and the reality running on parallel lines—or superimposed, like a—what did they call it—a palimpsest.

Then came the scene of the midnight burial of the victim on the north side of the church, the grave dug by her lover and a servant while the gargoyle monsters of men's macabre imagination grinned down at them from the church roof; the wedding; and the haunting of the bride on her honeymoon and after to the end.

The last shot of all showed the triumphant figure of Vashti standing on the terrace of the great house at nightfall, her long black hair streaming like a banner in the wind, her wild laughter ringing through the theatre until it became a part of the wailing of the storm, and her body disintegrated before their eyes into a whirling column of dead leaves.

There was a moment of profound silence which was a greater tribute to the picture than the roar of applause that followed.

As the lights went up Collier looked at his wife and saw that she had been crying.

As they made their way out through the foyer he overheard some of the comments of the audience.

"Great direction."

"Did you notice that the shadows of the cloaked figure of the informer whispering to Hopkins at the inn and of Delia trying on her wedding-dress were identical? A neat touch."

"Wasn't it horrible when that black thing slithered off the bed?"

"I think the worst bit was when she looked at her reflection in the glass and saw all that long black hair instead of her own fair curls. My dear! I nearly screamed."

"The two women were good, but so was Latimer. He contrived to make the part sympathetic—and it might not have been. The look on his face. Yes, the chap can act."

"Wasn't there some trouble while they were on location? Somebody died, or something."

As the audience dispersed, Evan Hughes, in the dress circle bar, was scribbling a message to be cabled to Latimer:

> "Success assured. Wish you were here to collect bouquets. Love and all the best from all here. Evan."

Rosamund Harper, leaning over his shoulder, said, "Love from Vashti."

"No."

Rosamund was a good trooper, but she couldn't understand. She had a look of Ida Condamine, and that was why Stephen had chosen her to play the part. The little Welshman knew that likeness had been a source of pain to his friend throughout the making of the picture. Stephen had suffered. He had been glad to get away, even at the cost of missing the hard-won applause that had always meant so much to him.

The night before Stephen sailed he had said, "I wanted to work in England, to make English films, I've a feeling that I shan't be much good in Hollywood. But if I stay here Ida will go on haunting me. That's why I have to go." He tried to laugh. "Witches can't cross running water."

THE END